THE MARQUESS MOVE

THE WHITMORELANDS
BOOK TWO

VALERIE BOWMAN

JUNE THIRD ENTERPRISES, LLC

The Marquess Move, copyright © 2023 by June Third Enterprises, LLC.

Print edition ISBN: 978-1-7368417-9-2

Digital edition ISBN: 978-1-7368417-8-5

Book Cover Design © Lyndsey Llewellen at Llewellen Designs.

For my lovely friend Michelle Dawnn.
It's such a joy to know you.

She's a maid with big dreams.

A dutiful lady's maid, Miss Madeline Atwood knows precisely what her future holds: countless nights of dressing her mistress in silk gowns, pinning her hair in elegant curls, and selecting the perfect pair of slippers before sending her off to the ball. But Madeline harbors a secret dream. Just once, *she'd* like to be the one who attends the grand party— and tonight could be her chance. All she needs to do is borrow her mistress's cast-off dress and sneak downstairs during the Twelfth Night Ball…

He's no prince charming.

Lord Justin Whitmoreland, Marquess of Whitmore, is a confirmed bachelor for good reason, and none of the eligible young ladies in London has even tempted him to change his mind about marriage. But after sharing one sensuous dance with a mystery woman, he finds himself looking for her around every street corner and in every ballroom. The very last place he expects his mystery woman to turn up is under his own roof.

Can midnight work some magic?

When Madeline is sacked from her job, Justin's meddling sister hires her as her new lady's maid. Which would be well and good if they didn't have to face temptation every day— and every night. Justin would have to be the worst kind of scoundrel to trifle with a woman in his employ, and Madeline believes she has zero chance of capturing a marquess's heart…so why is it so difficult for them to resist stealing private moments together? It's the most improbable of matches, but if the slipper fits…

CHAPTER ONE

London, Twelfth Night, 1814, The Earl of Hazelton's Town House

Madeline Atwood had two choices. She could rush back up the stairs, ask Anna to help her remove the stolen ballgown, replace the pilfered slippers and carry on as before, no one the wiser. Or she could continue her descent to the ballroom, where there was music and dancing and her *one* chance to fulfill her life-long dream. One magical night when she could pretend she was a debutante at a grand London ball.

Maddie peered over the servants' staircase. No one was there. *Thank goodness.* Now was her chance. The other servants were down in the kitchens preparing copious amounts of food. Or they were scattered about the rooms of Lord Hazelton's town house, catering to the two hundred guests who were enjoying themselves at the Hazeltons' annual Twelfth Night Ball.

Maddie glanced down at herself. She was wearing a sapphire ballgown that (thankfully) fit her perfectly and white satin slippers with blue satin bows on the tips. The slippers were too large, but she would make do. Her friend, Anna, had helped her twist her blond hair into a chignon, though Maddie had not been brave enough to pilfer any jewelry from Lady Henrietta's collection. She was already taking too much of a chance as it was.

Maddie took a deep, shaky breath. If she continued and was found out, she'd be risking everything she'd worked for these three past years. Molly was depending on her. Dear sweet Molly, seventeen years old. Out in the country living with Mrs. Halifax, who'd taken in the sisters after Papa's untimely death and the subsequent nightmare they'd endured. Molly needed Maddie to provide for her. She was all her younger sister had. The day Papa had passed away, his throat so ravaged by consumption, he'd barely been able to speak.

"*Take care of your sister, Madeline,*" he'd croaked.

"*I will, Papa. I promise.*"

And then Maddie had gone and done something that had not only compromised Molly's future, but her own. Which was why at the age of one and twenty, Maddie, the elder daughter of a baron, was working as a lady's maid for one Lady Henrietta Hazelton in London, scrimping and saving every ha'penny to send back home to her sister.

Maddie peered down the staircase once more. A thrill of excitement shot through her. She shouldn't be here. She shouldn't be dressed this way. She shouldn't be contemplating what she was contemplating. But after three years of following the rules every second, she was about to burst. Tonight, she intended to take a chance, to have a bit of fun. Just a small taste of the life she'd always thought would be hers until it all went wrong.

What she was about to do was stupid and selfish. But if she had to endure one more day in the drudgery of service without anything exciting, or even mildly out of the ordinary, she'd go mad. There was no choice, really. She already knew what she would do. She had known it since the moment she'd woken up this morning with her outlandish idea lodged in her brain and whispered it to Anna in the early, cold, dark moments before they slid from bed and began their chores. Maddie was going to sneak into her employer's ball and pretend to be a guest.

CHAPTER TWO

Justin Whitmoreland, the Marquess of Whitmore, was bored. He was always bored at *ton* events and this one was *particularly* boring. Hazelton's Twelfth Night Ball was an annual affair attended by nearly everyone in London. Justin was here for only one reason, however. To assist his closest friend, Sebastian, the Duke of Edgefield, who *happened* to be unhappily married to Justin's sister, Veronica.

Edgefield had asked Justin to meet him here to stave off the gossip as to why Veronica wasn't in attendance. As a duke with a prominent role in Parliament, Sebastian was required to attend such affairs. But without his duchess at his side, there would be questions. The lie was more plausible when Sebastian wasn't the only one spreading it—Veronica was feeling poorly…for the *second* Twelfth Night in a row.

Thankfully, Sebastian had promised that all Justin need do was mingle for an hour, mention to as many people as possible that Veronica had unfortunately fallen ill again —*rotten luck, that!*—and then he could take his leave. His duty to Edgefield fulfilled, Justin would be free to go to one of his favored gaming hells and spend the remainder of the evening engaged in much more pleasurable pursuits.

He didn't have much longer for pleasurable pursuits. This would be his final Season as a bachelor. He intended to make the most of it. Next year, his eighteen-year-old twin sisters would come to town to prepare for their debuts. He adored his sisters, all three of them, and he would do anything for them, but there was no doubt the twins' presence would require a significant change to his normally profligate schedule. He would be expected to squire them about town and eventually choose husbands for both of them, with their approval, of course. He had no illusions that his headstrong sisters would not be entirely involved in selecting their own husbands. He wouldn't have it any other way. He wanted all three of them happy. He even held out hope of Veronica and Edgefield reconciling. Though *that* was taking much longer than expected.

Fiercely loyal, Justin had a soft spot for his family and friends, which was precisely why he was here at this excruciatingly boring ball tonight, helping Edgefield pretend to be happily married. In fact, Justin had been here nearly a quarter of an hour already, though he had yet to locate his friend in the crush.

Justin expelled his breath. By God, the ball was even more crowded than last year...filled with marriage-minded misses and their mothers. The Season was not yet underway, so the ladies of the *ton* used Hazelton's ball as their one opportunity to march their darlings under the eyes of perspective grooms before it began.

Justin had already dodged half a dozen such mamas, their prim little daughters standing demurely at their sides. He was a thirty-year-old bachelor marquess, a prime target for such duos.

He glanced up.

Blast.

Lady Hazelton herself and her horse-faced daughter Henrietta were headed directly toward him. He needed to remove himself. Quickly.

Turning and pushing through the throng, he made his way down the nearest corridor and into the last room on the right. He shut the door behind him and pressed his back against it, closing his eyes and breathing a sigh of relief.

He'd narrowly escaped. Lady Hazelton and Henrietta were one of the most strident pairs he'd encountered. Insistent, loud, and not given to graciously accepting polite refusals of their requests. Justin made it a habit to keep from their sight.

"That was close," he murmured to himself, releasing a deep sigh into the empty, darkened room.

"What was close?" a lively female voice asked.

CHAPTER THREE

Maddie immediately regretted the words that had flown from her lips. Molly always said she was too quick to speak at times. She certainly had spoken too quickly one very important time in particular. She *should* have remained hidden by the potted palm she'd jumped behind when the door to the drawing room opened. She *should* have remained silent.

She'd been brave enough to descend the servants' staircase, lift the skirts of her pilfered blue ballgown, and tiptoe down the corridor toward the grand ballroom, but then a pair of footmen had come round the corner, and she'd fled into the first room she found.

A drawing room. A thankfully *empty* drawing room. She'd been trying to work up the nerve to continue with her plan ever since. She'd nearly convinced herself to do the intelligent thing and scurry back abovestairs with her tail between her legs when the door swung open, and a gentleman had rushed in.

"Pardon me," the man said, pushing himself off the door and taking a step toward her. His voice was deep and memorable. It sent a pleasurable tremor down her spine. "I didn't realize anyone was here."

"I'm not supposed to be here," she admitted, mostly because she couldn't think of anything else to say.

She couldn't help but look at him. A brace of candles sat atop the mantel close to where Maddie stood. They illuminated the room enough to allow her to slowly size him up. He *had* to be a guest. He was dressed in formal evening attire, mostly black, with a white waistcoat, shirtfront, and cravat. Well-cut and made with the finest of fabrics. As a lady's maid, she had an eye for such things. His clothes were no doubt more expensive than the entirety of Maddie's worldly possessions. He was tall and ridiculously fit, with dark-brown hair and obsidian eyes that were returning her gaze with interest. A sigh escaped her lips. He was the exact sort of handsome gentleman she'd imagined dancing with.

"Why aren't you supposed to be here?" he asked, a dark brow arching over one eye. "Are you hiding from the party too?"

No. The exact opposite, actually. She longed to be out at the party. But she was having second thoughts. What if one of the servants recognized her in the ballroom? Anna knew her secret, but no one else did. Maddie had counted on the others being too busy to look at her, just another party guest, but it would only take one servant recognizing her to ruin her plan. "I am hiding," she admitted, because at least that much was true, and she sensed the handsome gentleman was waiting for a reply.

"Why?" he asked, taking another step toward her, his brow furrowed in confusion.

"Why are *you* hiding in here?" she asked instead of answering him. She was truly curious to know the answer. A man this good-looking would be popular at an affair such as this. He must have a good reason for sneaking off.

"Because I detest these sorts of things," he replied. The hint of a smile quirked up his lips, and she loved that she'd been the one to put it there.

"You don't like to dance?" It ought to be against the law for a man that handsome to refuse to take to the dance floor.

"Dancing is for married men, lovesick fools, and fops," he replied, slowly shaking his head.

"I see," she replied, before asking him another question that was sure to elicit another negative response. For some reason, she was enjoying prodding him. "You do not like to mingle?" She'd so longed to be a carefree party guest, but she supposed not everyone felt the same.

"Not at all." He chuckled this time.

"How do you feel about eating *hors d'oeuvres?*" she ventured, suppressing her smile.

He shrugged. "Mostly indifferent, I'm afraid."

"So, you don't care for fun then?" She nearly laughed but stopped herself.

"Not the sort of fun found at an event such as this," he drawled.

"But if you don't like to dance, mingle, or consume *hors d'oeuvres*, then why are you here?" Oh, dear. Maddie frowned as an unwelcome thought occurred to her. Perhaps he was a rake...perhaps he had arranged an amorous liaison...and perhaps she walked right into the middle of it. Her voice had gone a little breathless at the end there, but the thought of him meeting another woman was oddly provoking.

A smile spread across his face, making him even more handsome, if that was possible. He moved even closer to her. He was standing only two paces away. He was quite tall and the scent of his obviously expensive, yet sparingly applied cologne made her knees wobble.

She was in over her head. She needed to leave. Soon.

"I am doing a favor...for a friend," he told her.

Now *that* was interesting. Perhaps he wasn't a rake after all. He certainly looked like one, but she'd be lying if she said she wasn't relieved. "What sort of favor?" she asked, cocking her head to the side. "Are you close with Lord Hazelton?" Because if he was, she needed to leave immediately. She should not be consorting with anyone who might mention their encounter to her employer.

The handsome gentleman smiled again, and she briefly wished he would always smile. "No. I barely know him," he said.

She allowed her shoulders to relax. "Thank goodness," she said before she had a chance to think better of it.

He narrowed his eyes at her. "May I ask your name?"

Oh, no. She needed to get out of here. Perhaps he wasn't a rake, but he was disordering her thoughts, and she needed to keep her wits about her if she was going to pull off this mad plan. At some point during this remarkable conversation with this outrageously handsome man, she'd found the courage she'd needed and now she was anxious to get on with it.

"You may ask, but I cannot share it. In fact, I must go." She hurried past him to the door and cracked it open, peeking out, trying to ignore the alluring scent of sandalwood that met her nostrils as she passed him.

"You are in a hurry?" His voice came from behind her this time.

"Yes," she replied. "I don't have much time to accomplish my goal." Thank goodness. The way was clear. She would make her way down the corridor and blend into the sizable crowd. Surely, no one would notice one more lady in the crush. She opened the door wider. "Good night, Mr...."

"Mr.?" he said as if it were a question.

Oh, no. Was he *not* a mister? *Was he a lord?* Good heavens. She truly must leave immediately. She had no business messing about with lords. Though no doubt the ballroom was lousy with them. "My apologies, I thought—"

"Mr. Whitland," he said quickly. "But wait. Where are you going? What is your goal?"

She stopped and glanced back at him. The man was gorgeous, to be certain, and apparently he *was* a mister—thank heavens—but he'd already indicated he didn't enjoy dancing. More's the pity. She needed to find a gentleman who liked to dance...and quickly.

"To dance with a handsome gentleman at the ball," she announced over her shoulder, and she couldn't resist sending him a grin. She paused for a moment before tapping a gloved finger to her cheek and adding something that had just occurred to her. "And perhaps eat an *hors d'oeuvre* or two." And with that, she shot him a wink and slipped from the room, even though a part of her wanted to stay.

CHAPTER FOUR

Justin watched the space where the young lady had just been. For a moment, he wondered if the entire encounter with her had been nothing more than a figment of his imagination. It had been so odd. And he wasn't entirely certain he'd heard her correctly. Had she said her goal was to dance with a handsome gentleman at a ball? That was a first. He'd never heard anyone say such a thing. No one except his younger sister Jessica, who couldn't wait to make her debut.

But if the woman he'd just encountered was a debutante, what was she doing in here alone? Where was her mother? Besides, usually when he encountered debutantes who wanted to dance, they were looking to make *him* their part-ner. But this young woman hadn't seemed to know who he was. She appeared solely interested in dancing and in a hurry to quit his company.

Justin absently scratched his chin, still staring at the doorway. Who was she? She was certainly pretty. She had thick blond hair, irrepressible dimples, and cornflower blue eyes that sparkled with mischief. And her voice had been happy and full of life. He'd never wanted to prolong an acquaintance with a debutante, but he had to admit he'd been disappointed when she left the room. Odd. All of it. And she wasn't even an acquaintance, was she? She hadn't so much as given him a name. In fact, she'd *refused* to tell him her name.

He wanted to follow her. That was a first as well. The thought surprised him. There was something captivating about her. Of course, he wasn't interested in dancing. Justin never wanted to dance, but for some reason he couldn't explain, he wanted to see *her* dance. Perhaps only to learn whether she'd accomplished the goal she'd seemed so intent upon.

Justin shook his head and rubbed at his forehead with a knuckle. He was being absurd. Why did he care about a fanciful young lady's desire to dance? He had his own goal tonight, and it involved finding Edgefield, spreading word of his sister's nonexistent illness, and getting the hell out of this ball filled with married couples and boring little innocents.

Though, now that he thought on it, the young woman he'd just encountered hadn't bored him. That was a first too. She looked slightly older than most of the debutantes, and she didn't have a mother with her. Was she a debutante? Perhaps she merely didn't want anyone to know she'd been in a room alone with a man. He couldn't blame her for that. Reputations were easily lost with less fodder.

If she *was* a debutante, perhaps she'd yet to make her debut. But that made little sense. She wouldn't be at the ball if she hadn't made her debut. And she'd said she wasn't supposed to be in the drawing room. He'd assumed that was only because she should be out in the crowd with her mama keeping a close eye on her.

But why had she refused to give him her name? In fairness, he hadn't told her his name either. Not his real one, at least. When she'd declined to reveal her name, he'd decided to keep his identity secret as well for some reason. He hadn't mentioned that he was a marquess and not just a mister. She'd assumed he was a mister so easily, he hadn't wanted to disabuse her of the notion. It was rare that a debutante wouldn't know who he was. He wasn't given to tossing his title about, but somehow they *all* seemed to know who he was...not that he relished it. On the contrary, it was refreshing to find a debutante who didn't know him. *Quite* refreshing, actually.

Justin shook his head again. What was the matter with him? It was unlike him, spending so much time wondering about a young woman. Any young woman, debutante or not. He usually avoided such innocents like a case of the pox. He preferred the more experienced women he met at the gaming hells around London. Women who were used to pleasure and knew how to give and receive it. Oh, he would have to marry, eventually, he knew that. He already had a sound plan for it. He intended to find a woman who wanted his title and would bear him an heir, but who didn't care one whit about him. *That* was the secret to a marriage free from pain and disappointment. In the meantime, he would find his pleasure in dalliances at the hells.

Justin scrubbed a hand through his hair. The unexpected encounter with the young woman who wanted to dance had distracted him long enough. He should return to the ballroom, find Edgefield, look for a few more people to inform of Veronica's unfortunate illness, and then get on with his night. He exited the drawing room, closing the door behind him and putting thoughts of the pretty young blond woman firmly from his mind.

The ballroom was just as he'd left it, filled with people and music and laughter. And this time, Lady Hazelton and Henrietta were thankfully nowhere to be found. He politely nodded to a few acquaintances and stopped to speak briefly with some friends, who obligingly asked after Veronica's health. As he made his way through the crush, he kept an eye out for Edgefield...and if he spotted the blond woman, so be it.

Justin decided to tour the perimeter of the room. He had no sooner made his way toward the closest wall when he spied Edgefield in a small group that included Lord Hazelton, by the double doors at the front of the room. Justin changed his course immediately.

"Ah, Whitmore," Edgefield said the moment he looked up and saw Justin striding toward him. "Good to see you." The duke turned to the group he was with. "I was just telling Hazelton here that Veronica isn't feeling well this evening."

"That's right," Justin smoothly interjected, shaking his head as if it were a shame. "My dear sister is under the weather again. I swear there must be something about the Christmastide season that doesn't agree with her."

"She sends her regrets, of course," Edgefield added.

Lord Hazelton eyed Edgefield warily. "How unfortunate. I must ask Lady Hazelton to stop by your town house to see if Her Grace needs anything."

"Nonsense," Edgefield replied, a fake smile plastered on his face. Justin knew that inside Edgefield was wishing he could punch Hazelton in the gut. "She has me and a team of maids at the ready. She's been asleep most of the day. I'm certain she'll be fit in no time."

"Very well," Hazelton allowed, still eyeing Edgefield with a look that indicated in no uncertain terms he didn't believe a word the duke had said.

Justin returned Hazelton's careful stare. The earl clearly knew the rumors that Veronica had left Edgefield barely two months after their wedding nearly eighteen months ago. She'd fled to their country house and not been back. London had been rife with chatter about her marriage ever since.

Both Edgefield and Veronica were absurdly stubborn and refused to listen to reason, and so they remained at odds. Justin could only hope they made up soon. He doubted the *ton* would believe his lies for a third year.

As the group's conversation switched to another topic, Justin scoured the ballroom for a head of blond hair and a sapphire gown. He found no trace. He frowned, wondering for the dozenth time why he was looking.

Soon, Hazelton and his friends drifted off to speak to other guests, and Justin was left alone with Edgefield.

"Thank you," Edgefield said, expelling his breath, his shoulders relaxing.

"You're quite welcome," Justin replied. "Besides Hazelton, I spoke to the Rothchilds, Lord and Lady Pembroke, and the Cranberrys."

Edgefield nodded. "Excellent."

"Is there anyone else you'd like me to inform of my dear sister's poor health before I take my leave?"

"No," Edgefield said with a shake of the head. "That should suffice."

"You know you'll need to speak to Veronica eventually. This cannot go on forever."

"Tell that to your stubborn sister," Edgefield replied with a tight smile.

Justin rolled his eyes. Sebastian and Veronica were far too alike, which made them both an excellent match and formidable enemies when they so chose.

"Will I see you later, at the club?" Justin asked to change the subject. He'd learned long ago it did little good to try to convince either Sebastian or Veronica to see reason.

"Yes. I intend to win back the fifty pounds you stole from me last night."

"I think you mean you plan to lose fifty more to me tonight," Justin replied with a wink. The two friends often bet on hands of cards, and neither was up for long before the other won back his money. They'd been winning and losing the same fifty pounds for years. "At any rate, I'll stop to thank Lady Hazelton for her hospitality, and then I'll be going," Justin said.

Edgefield nodded and drifted off into the crowd, most likely to talk to some of the other members of Parliament about an upcoming bill or some other boring nonsense. Sebastian took his duties seriously. As a duke, he had to. Justin was far less inclined. He might be a marquess, but he'd yet to settle into the years of obligation men in his position seemed destined for. There would be plenty of time for that later...when he stopped having so much bloody fun.

Justin soon located his hostess and offered the obligatory thanks. He might be a profligate rake, but his mother had drilled manners and decorum into him from the moment he was born. He turned to make his way out the doors toward the foyer. As he went, he pulled his gold timepiece from the inside pocket of his coat and consulted it. Excellent. He could be at his favorite hell within twenty minutes if the streets weren't crowded.

But instead of continuing toward the door, he found himself...stopping. Stopping, turning, and looking around for...her. The blond woman from the drawing room. He took a spot along the edge of the dance floor and scanned the crowd. Had she found her handsome gentleman? Was she dancing? If he saw her, that would be enough, and he would leave. But even as his gaze searched the dance floor, he chastised himself. Why the hell did he care if a complete stranger got her dance? He didn't even know who she was. And he certainly would *not* ask anyone to tell him her name. That would only cause gossip. He was *leaving*.

He turned on his heel. But just before he made it to the doors, he couldn't help but glance back *one* more time...

As if the light had caught it solely for his eye, a swath of sapphire satin illuminated on the far side of the room. It was paired with a head full of blond hair and a lovely profile that had been etched into his memory. It was her. He'd found her. She was not on the dance floor, however. Instead, she stood on the far side of the dancing, and she seemed to be…in an argument with a man.

The middle-aged man wore a bright green coat atop ungodly peacock-blue pantaloons. He was jabbing a large finger toward the dance floor while the blond lady stood with her gloved hands on her hips and an animated expression on her face, which included a decided frown. Justin watched in silence for a few more moments until the peacock grabbed the lady's arm and pulled her along behind him toward the dancing.

Justin didn't stop to think. He pushed through the crowd and strode forcefully past the dancers to make his way to her side.

"I don't care to dance with you, my lord," she was saying while tugging against the older man's obviously too-strong grip.

The peacock wasn't listening. He continued to pull her toward the dance floor.

Justin stepped directly into Peacock's path, where he squared his shoulders and pushed the flat of one hand hard against the man's puffed-out chest. "I believe the young lady said she's not interested in a dance with you." His voice was deep and gruff, intended for absolutely no misinterpretation on Peacock's part.

"Who are you?" the man asked brusquely, giving Justin a look intended to burn through him.

Justin returned his penetrating gaze. The man was half a foot shorter than him and though quite a bit heavier, Justin had no doubt his years spent mastering the art of fencing, specifically an *esquive,* would send this oaf crashing to the floor if he attempted to lunge at him.

"Who are *you?*" Justin demanded, glancing around. Where in the world was this young woman's mother? She wasn't doing a very good job of chaperoning her charge tonight.

"I'm Lord Julington," the man replied, narrowing his eyes on Justin.

Justin crossed his arms over his chest and glowered at Lord Julington. "Suffice it to say, *I'm* someone who doesn't take kindly to seeing ladies forced into unwanted dances."

The man attempted to push past Justin. "Get out of my way. This is none of your concern."

Justin stopped him with an arm to his throat. "I'm about to make it my concern if you don't unhand this lady immediately."

The man released the young woman's arm but continued to glare at Justin. "I don't believe I caught your name, Sir," he snarled through clenched teeth.

"I don't believe I provided it," Justin replied, stepping back and straightening his coat.

Justin glanced around briefly. The partygoers nearest to their little trio had stopped talking and dancing and were standing in a semicircle, staring at them. They had caused a scene. From the corner of his eye, Justin spied Lord Hazelton himself marching toward them.

The next sound Justin heard was the lady's inhaled breath and a sharp squeak. He glanced at her. Stark terror flashed in her eyes before she turned on her heel and rushed away in the opposite direction.

CHAPTER FIVE

Maddie slammed the door to the drawing room behind her. She rushed to the far end of the room, pacing and wringing her hands. Oh, no. Had Lord Hazelton seen her? She didn't think so, but she couldn't be certain. All she knew was that she'd fled the moment her employer had walked in her direction.

This was precisely why she shouldn't have taken this chance tonight. It all sounded like a lark when one was giggling about it with Anna in the wee hours, but it was much less fun when one was hiding in a drawing room wearing stolen clothing, hoping that one's employer didn't find her.

No. No. No. This had all been a mistake. There would be no dance with a handsome gentleman at a ball. She'd been a fool to think she could manage it. She'd just wait until the corridor was empty and then she'd sneak back upstairs, surreptitiously return the clothing, and be done with this entire idiotic plot. And she—

The door to the drawing room swung open and Maddie's heart stopped. But it quickly started again when Mr. Whitland poked in his head. He saw her, then stepped inside and closed the door behind him.

He was alone. Thank heavens. She expelled her pent-up breath in a rush, beyond grateful for her good fortune.

"There you are," he said in his affable tone from earlier, quite unlike the tone with which he'd addressed Lord Julington.

"I...I'm sorry." Her voice faltered. "I wasn't...feeling well." She lifted her chin. There. Wasn't that what debutantes always said? Lady Henrietta tended to, at least.

"I'm sorry to hear that," Mr. Whitland replied. "I hope you haven't allowed your unfortunate encounter with that fool Julington to stop you from having your dance."

"Oh, er, yes. Yes, indeed. I'm no longer interested in dancing," she declared. "In fact, I'm just about to leave...the ballroom. Er...leave the party." She closed her eyes briefly, chiding herself for the ridiculously high pitch to her voice. She squeaked when she was nervous.

"Where is your mother?" Mr. Whitland asked next, his eyes narrowing on her. "Allow me to escort you to her."

Fear streaked through Maddie's chest again. "I, er, that is to say... I—"

"My apologies," he interjected. "I didn't intend to be forward. Only, it seems to me that you're lacking a chaperone and—"

"Thank you for your help, Mr. Whitland. But I must go." She grabbed her skirts and made to step around him.

"Wait." He held out a hand to her. "I'm uncertain if I qualify, but I'm willing to dance if you would still care to."

Maddie froze. A tentative smile curled her lips. Did she *dare* take him up on the offer? The strains of a waltz were barely audible. Anyone might walk into the room at any moment, including Lord Hazelton himself. For all she knew, Lord Julington was still looking for her. But none of it mattered. Her heart pounded and excitement shot through her middle. She would be a churl and a fool to allow this opportunity to pass. It was so...perfect. They could dance here, in this room, with no prying eyes. Would she still care to dance? Yes, indeed. She *would* care to. Though she was entirely certain that she shouldn't. She turned and eyed Mr. Whitland carefully.

"Come on," he added, tugging his bottom lip with his straight white teeth in an utterly irresistible, vulnerable way that made her belly flip. "Try it. I'm told I'm not the *worst* dancer in the world."

She bit her lip, quite willing to take him up on the offer but still a bit hesitant. "I thought you said only lovesick fools and fops dance?"

"And married men," he replied with a sigh. "I am none of those things, but I am willing to make an exception...for a beautiful woman who wishes to dance."

Oh, well, *that* was charming.

Maddie tentatively reached out and placed her hand on his. He pulled her into his arms, enveloping her in his warmth, the scent of sandalwood stronger so near him. He began the steps of the waltz, in perfect time to the music still drifting into the room. One, two, three. One, two, three. They turned in a circle in the large space between the sideboard and the settee. She looked up into his dark eyes and smiled at him, one hand clasped in his, the other resting upon his strong, wide shoulder.

And then she danced, just as her mother had taught her all those years ago. Just as she'd taught Molly. And for those few minutes as the waltz played, it was magical, and Maddie was actually a debutante dancing at a grand London ball, just as she'd always imagined. She closed her eyes and breathed in the moment's magic, knowing full well she would never have the opportunity again.

After several moments had passed, and she'd reopened her eyes, Mr. Whitland spoke. "So, what happened out there with Lord Julington?"

Her smile disappeared, and Maddie fought her shudder. But she had to be careful in her response. "He asked me to dance, and I refused."

"Wasn't quite handsome enough for you?" Mr. Whitland prodded with a smile.

She shook her head. "He was far too insistent, actually. I regret you had to involve yourself in that unfortunate encounter. Thank you for your assistance, by the by."

"Don't worry. After I explained what had happened, Lord Hazelton insisted he leave. You won't have to worry about Julington again tonight."

A hint of relief washed over her at that news, but it was quickly followed by more apprehension. She bit her lip, eyeing Mr. Whitland warily. "What exactly did you tell Lord Hazelton?" she asked, forcing herself not to wince.

They continued to dance as Mr. Whitland replied, "Only that Lord Julington had been so rude to a female guest, so insistent upon a dance, that the young lady had run off."

"Did Lord Hazelton...?" She cleared her throat and hoped her squeak didn't return. "Ask my name?"

"No," Mr. Whitland replied with a grin, "which was fortunate since I didn't have a name to give him."

Nodding, she breathed a sigh of relief and smiled widely at him. "Of course not."

The music stopped and Mr. Whitland brought their dance to an end, but his fingers lingered on her waist. She didn't remove her hand from his shoulder either. She tipped back her head to look up at him. He gazed down at her intently and slowly—oh, so slowly—lowered his head. He was going to kiss her. She knew it. And she wanted him to. After all, sharing a kiss with a handsome gentleman at a ball was her *second* dream. One she had barely even acknowledged to herself. It had been too much to hope for when she'd planned tonight, but now, now, the most handsome gentleman she'd seen at the ball had not only danced with her...he was poised to kiss her too. She leaned up on her tiptoes to meet him halfway.

Voices sounded in the corridor, breaking the spell, and Maddie quickly scrambled away from him. The voices were so close they sounded as if their owners might enter the room. She twirled desperately in a circle, searching for the best hiding place. The potted palm wasn't big enough. Instead, she scurried behind the velvet blue drapes. She hovered there, trying to hold her breath, when the voices passed the drawing room.

Thank heavens. Sucking air into her lungs, she pressed a hand to her chest and said another brief prayer. *That* had been far too close. She'd taken too much of a risk. A dance was one thing, but a kiss was a step too far. What if those people had opened the door and found her in a compromising position with a man she didn't even know? She shuddered to think about what might have happened. She'd been a complete fool to play this game. She had to go. Her playacting was over. For good.

Mr. Whitland's footsteps drew near. He pulled back the drapes. His eyes narrowed on her, and he was grinning at her as if she'd amused him. "It's all right. You can come out."

She gave him a tentative smile, suddenly quite aware of how foolish she must look hiding behind curtains. No use explaining. He probably assumed she was worried about her reputation and that was mostly true. She nodded as she stepped out into the room and then tiptoed to the door and peeked out. The corridor was empty. "I must go," she breathed.

She turned to look at him one last time. He had an

inscrutable expression on his face. Dare she hope there was a bit of disappointment in it?

"Please, tell me your name," he requested, in such a hopeful voice her heart flipped.

If she were clever, she would make up a name. But something inside her prodded her to tell him the truth. It would be completely improper for him to call her by her Christian name, and yet she found herself saying breathlessly, "Madeline. My name is Madeline."

And with that, she flew from the room. She'd had her dance. It was time to return to her real life.

CHAPTER SIX

London, Twelfth Night, 1815, The Earl of Hazelton's Town House

This year, instead of arriving solo, Justin arrived at Hazelton's Twelfth Night Ball with his entire family in tow. Well, all of them save Veronica. She was coming with her husband finally. Over the Christmastide holiday, Veronica and Edgefield had managed to put their disagreement to rights—with a bit of help from the rest of the Whitmoreland family. Mama, Grandpapa, Grandmama, and the twins, Jessica and Elizabeth, had all insisted on coming to the Twelfth Night Ball to see the couple happily reunited. Even though the twins weren't officially out yet, they'd come too. Grandpapa's title as a duke would shield them from any gossip.

Justin had merely come to support his family. He was doing his duty. Or so he told himself for the hundredth time as he escorted his mother into the ballroom on his arm. It had been a year. One year since he'd been in this same house and shared a dance with a young lady he hadn't been able to put from his mind since.

It made no sense. He *never* spared so much as a second thought for any young lady, and he certainly didn't think of any of them *often*. Yet, Madeline—the only name he had to go by—had come up in his thoughts a disturbing number of times over the last twelve months. In fact, if he was being honest with himself, he would admit that he'd spent the entire last Season searching every crowd for her. Only to be repeatedly disappointed. He'd even considered asking about her. But where would he begin and who would he ask? He didn't have her surname. Not to mention that his asking after a debutante would do nothing but spark gossip.

The closest he'd come to mentioning her to anyone was a discussion earlier this afternoon with Edgefield. Justin had advised his friend that he would be looking for someone—a young lady—at the ball tonight. Justin hoped he didn't live to regret it now that Edgefield and Veronica were back together. If Edgefield mentioned to Veronica—or worse, Mama or Jessica—that he was in search of a certain young lady, he'd never have a moment's peace.

But it was too late now, he reckoned as he scanned the ballroom. It was ludicrous to hope he'd find her, of course. Not only did he have no earthly idea who she was, there was certainly no guarantee that she'd be attending the ball again this year. But Hazelton's Twelfth Night Ball was the one place he'd seen her before, and he couldn't help that a small part of him held out hope he'd find her here again.

He installed his family along the sidelines of the dancing and stood impatiently, surveying the crowd. He was looking for a sapphire dress, which was foolish. What were the odds she'd be wearing sapphire again?

"It's not a question of if, Eliza, it's a necessity," Mama was saying to his sister, Elizabeth.

Elizabeth, who had always scorned social affairs and fripperies in favor of reading books and scribbling in her journal, rolled her eyes. "But I don't *need* a lady's maid, Mama. It's entirely unnecessary."

"Nonsense," Mama replied. "When the Season begins, who'll help you with your clothing, jewelry, and hair?"

"Jessa's maid can button my gowns. I don't need jewelry, and I cannot stand to have my hair up."

Mama pressed a hand to her throat. "You cannot be serious, child. You cannot go to social affairs with your hair down. It's indecent."

"Decency is overrated," Eliza replied.

Justin had to turn his laugh into a cough and look away from his mother's narrow-eyed glare. Mama and Eliza had been having this argument for several weeks now and it didn't look as if either intended to change her stance. Eliza was firmly set on *not* employing a lady's maid, and Mama was equally intent upon ensuring she had one.

On any other evening, Justin might have been amused by his family's squabble, but tonight he had no intention of listening to the ongoing debate. He preferred to stroll around the ballroom to see if he recognized…anyone. Perhaps take a slight detour into a certain drawing room?

"I'll be back shortly," he informed the group, though he doubted any of them heard him as they were all in a merry argument about the merits and necessity of lady's maids. Jessica, who was greatly looking forward to her Season, was quite vocal on the subject and firmly on Mama's side.

His family's spirited discussion was the perfect cover under which Justin could slip away unnoticed. He wasted no time taking a turn around the room, one intended to look quite casual but was anything but. He found himself holding his breath time and again as he came upon a blond woman, but each time she turned around, he was disappointed. He'd gone the length of the room and back before he decided that however ludicrous the notion and however low the odds of her being there, he couldn't live with himself if he didn't at least *visit* the drawing room where they'd had their dance last year.

On his way, he was forced to dodge many debutantes looking hopeful that he'd ask them to dance. Why exactly had he thought it a good idea to attend this ball again? He usually avoided it like the plague, and this year he didn't even have the excuse that he was attending to help Edgefield spread the word about another one of Veronica's fake illnesses.

As for Veronica, when Justin passed the dance floor, his attention was drawn to the center where Edgefield and Veronica were gazing at each other lovingly, swaying together to the tune of a waltz. He smiled to himself. At least those two were back together again, as they should be. He'd never encountered a more maddeningly stubborn pair. Or a more well suited one.

Justin slipped from the ballroom into the corridor and down the hallway to the drawing room. He cursed himself a fool with each step. Of course, Madeline wouldn't be in the room. Of course, it would be empty. It was absurd to look.

Justin didn't realize he'd been holding his breath again until he opened the door of the drawing room to find...dark emptiness. Letting out his pent-up breath, he stepped inside, allowing the door to remain ajar. Should he check behind the curtains? No, that was ridiculous. Sticking his hands in his coat pockets, he kicked at the rug. It *had* been foolish to think she would be here. But still...the disappointment in his chest lingered.

Instead of leaving, he stepped farther into the room and rubbed the tip of his boot against the spot on the floor near the settee where he'd held her in his arms. He smiled to himself as he remembered the feel of her there as they danced. What was it about her that had so captivated him after only a few minutes' interaction? It was a good question and one that had plagued him all these months. She'd been... unexpected. Her demeanor, her words, her actions. Everything about her had been the exact opposite of what he encountered with most debutantes. She'd been unapologetic too. That was something he admired about anyone. She'd been lively where other debutantes always seemed to be attempting to win an award for being quiet and demure. Both of which drove him mad. His sisters weren't quiet and demure. He preferred ladies who spoke their mind and enjoyed themselves. Precisely as Madeline had seemed to.

Madeline had also been...mysterious, and he realized with some irony that part of his attraction to her was that she'd seemed completely unaffected by him. Normally, when a debutante encountered him at a ball, she endeavored to act charming or beguiling to cajole him into asking her to dance. Madeline, however, had rushed from the room the moment he'd indicated he didn't enjoy dancing. She'd been more interested in the dancing itself. And *that*—for some completely unknown reason—intrigued him. He hated that it was true, but there it was.

He blew out a breath and tipped back his head. Facing the ceiling, he closed his eyes for a moment, imagining the strains of the same waltz that had been playing during their dance last year and pretending he could feel her delicate gloved hand in his. She'd smelled like lilacs. He'd had his house filled with them all last spring.

Loud female voices sounded in the hallway, breaking the spell, just before his three sisters rushed into the room.

"There you are, Justin," Veronica exclaimed, glancing around the darkened room. "What are you doing in here?"

"*Trying* to have a moment of peace," he replied with a tight smile.

"In an empty drawing room?" Jessa asked, frowning.

"That's what makes it peaceful, Jessa, the emptiness," Eliza offered helpfully.

Justin crossed his arms over his chest and eyed his three sisters. He'd learned long ago that the best way to get them to stop asking questions was to ask questions of his own. "What are all of *you* doing here?"

"Looking for you, of course," Eliza replied with a shrug. Eliza was the most reasonable of his sisters. He doubted she'd come of her own accord. No doubt the forceful Veronica and her equally dogged associate Jessa had insisted Eliza accompany them. Eliza and Jessa may have been identical in likeness, but their personalities were far different. Jessa acted much more like Veronica, who loved fashion and Society and poking her nose into her brother's private affairs whenever possible.

"Edgefield told us you're hunting for a certain lady," Jessica blurted.

"Did he?" Justin arched a brow, inwardly sighed, and made a mental note to thank Edgefield later.

Veronica gave Jessica a condemning glare. "You're not supposed to *tell* him that."

"What do you mean?" Jessica replied, her brow furrowed. "You don't think he already knows he's looking for a lady?"

Veronica put the back of her hand to her forehead. "No. I meant you're not supposed to let him know *we* know he's looking for a lady. Now he'll refuse to tell us *anything*."

"I'm sorry to disappoint," Justin said, already moving back toward the door. "But there is obviously no lady here."

"I told you both this was a waste of time," Eliza drawled.

Good, sensible Eliza. She *had* been dragged along by the other two.

Justin had nearly made it to the still-open door when he glimpsed a light pink ballgown and the profile of none other than…Madeline standing in the corridor.

There she was, hovering outside the door. No figment of his imagination. Only, the moment he saw her, she was just as quickly gone. She scurried off in the opposite direction toward the back of the house.

Justin quickly turned to his sisters. "I have just recalled that I promised Hazelton I'd meet him in his study for a drink with some other chaps." And with that hasty excuse, he strode from the room.

Out in the corridor, he barely saw the last bit of pink satin round a corner toward the right. He nearly ran after her, intent on not letting her go this time without getting a surname. When he turned the corner, he was in the back of the house. He glanced around. The door to the servants' staircase was just closing. He frowned. Where was she going?

Without thinking, he followed her. He pushed open the door and glanced up to see pink satin wending its way up the staircase above him. With no more thought than before, he began climbing the stairs.

"Stop!" he called. "I must speak with you."

A small feminine gasp echoed from above, but her footsteps did indeed stop. He jogged up the last several steps to her.

She stood there looking lovely in a soft pink gown with tiny white rosebuds embroidered along the bodice. She was wearing long white gloves, a small white fur stole around her shoulders, and sparkling diamonds on her ears. She was as ethereal as he remembered. More so, perhaps, with her fine bones and bright blue eyes. She was blinking at him with a mixture of surprise and—dare he hope—delight on her face.

"Madeline," he breathed, coming to a stop in front of her, his breath only slightly elevated because of his climb. "I've…

you came to the drawing room?" It was an obvious and idiotic thing to say, but he was just so pleased with the fact that she had come. She'd been there. Right where he'd met her last year. His noisy sisters must have frightened her off.

Madeline swallowed and nodded. But she still said nothing. She glanced around as if worried they'd be discovered. He still did not know why she'd climbed up the servants' staircase. But now that he was standing here staring at her, he realized how, well, rude it all must seem to her.

"I must apologize," he began. "I hope I didn't...frighten you. I hope you're not unhappy that I wanted to speak with you."

Her bright blue eyes blinked, and she shook her head. "No...only..." She bit her lip in the charming way he well remembered from last year.

"Only what?" he prompted. She glanced about so frequently he was getting nervous too. Did she expect someone? He felt like an utter fool. He had no reason to follow her and no coherent thing to say to her now that he'd chased her and stopped her.

"Only, I'm...I must go," she said, her eyes still darting back and forth.

"Very well," he replied, feeling like an ass. He had no excuse for accosting this poor young woman. "But...I wanted to tell you something."

"What?" Her eyes went wide, and she looked at him hopefully, seeming on tenterhooks waiting for his pronouncement.

"I..." He licked his dry lips. "I couldn't stop thinking about you...all year."

A shy smile spread across her pretty face and her dimples made his knees weak. "I couldn't stop thinking of you either," she admitted in a whisper before whipping around to leave.

He frowned again. She'd thought of him too? Then why

was she in such a hurry to leave? "Wait." He searched his mind for *something* to say. Something to keep her in his presence for one moment more. "May I…may I ask your surname?"

She turned back to face him, and her mouth formed a wide O. "Oh, no," she exclaimed, shaking her head vehemently. "No."

Justin frowned. "No?"

He was debating whether he should ask her why, while telling himself he should simply take no for an answer and leave, when she grabbed him by the lapels of his black evening coat, pushed herself up on tiptoes and kissed him full on the mouth.

Only moments later, before he had a chance to react, let alone make the kiss good, she pushed away from him, gathered up her skirts and continued her flight up the stairs. "Good-bye, Mr. Whitland," she called, waving a gloved arm at him as if he were a sailor about to ship off. "It was nice to meet you. I do hope you have a lovely life."

CHAPTER SEVEN

Maddie rushed up to the tiny bedchamber she shared with Anna and scurried inside, shutting the door firmly behind her. Her breath came in harsh pants while her heart raced so quickly it hurt. She closed her eyes and recited a brief prayer. She hadn't been seen, thank heavens. A miracle. It had been madness, dashing through the house and rushing up the staircase, only to be stopped by the man she had been trying to find.

All these months, she'd been unable to forget her dance with Mr. Whitland. The dance had been magical. But it was also fanciful to keep thinking about it. She'd tried to put the entire episode behind her. But late at night, as she fell to sleep on her small cot, she closed her eyes and dreamed of waltzing with him, his strong arms locked around her, his dark eyes shining down on her, the quirk of a smile on his firmly molded lips. The smell of sandalwood and the hint of music in the air. She'd sigh and fall into a sated slumber.

But each morning she'd wake to the reality that she would never save enough money to bring her sister to town. The bit of money Maddie made was paid monthly and while she'd saved nearly every shilling, it would take her more than a lifetime to buy Molly gowns, let alone all the other things she would need to make her debut. She'd asked Lady Henrietta if she might take some of her old, discarded things, but the lady had refused, insisting the rubbish heap was a better place for the clothing than giving them to Maddie. It had physically hurt not to take the precious garments, but Maddie was no thief. She may have borrowed Lady Henrietta's clothing, shoes, and earbobs tonight, but she had every intention of giving them back in the same condition.

Maddie still cringed when she thought of the circumstances that had brought her and Molly to this fate. She'd been reckless. That had always been her problem. She followed her heart when she should have followed good sense. But she *had* spent the last year doing her best to concentrate on being an excellent maid to Lady Henrietta. Maddie had stopped doing whimsical things like trying to dance at parties. Over and over these last months, she'd reminded herself how selfish she'd been putting her sister's future at risk for a silly dance. But as the Twelfth Night Ball approached again this year, she thought about *him* more and more. She couldn't stop herself from wondering if he would return.

She also had made the mistake of mentioning the subject to Anna one too many times. Anna was adamant that she should dress up again—just once more—and go back to the drawing room to see if he came to find her.

"It will be so romantic," Anna had insisted, clasping her hands together near her ear. "Just imagine. What if *he's* been thinking about *you* all year too?"

Of course, Maddie had scoffed at such a notion. She'd never take such a risk again. Why in the world would a gentleman as handsome as Mr. Whitland give their inconsequential dance a second thought? She was certain he had not.

But as the night of the ball drew near, she'd been unable to stop thinking about it. *What if?* Those two words haunted her day and night. *What if* he was there? *What if* he did come looking for her? *What if* they danced again? Would it really be so horrible to check? She could be down and back in minutes, and if he wasn't there, well, then he'd never know she'd come looking for him, would he?

She'd made the final decision just this morning. She would do it. Just once more. She'd go into Lady Henrietta's rooms, pick out a gown, some slippers, and even a bit of jewelry this time, and go to the drawing room. Nowhere else. Not the ballroom. She'd never risk attracting that kind of attention again. It would be much less risky than what she'd done last year, showing her face in the ballroom, and nearly being seen by Lord Hazelton.

She'd done it. She'd picked out the lovely pink gown, one that Lady Henrietta detested, but Maddie thought was gorgeous. She'd slipped on a pair of too-large satin slippers, and she'd borrowed a pair of diamond earbobs that were no doubt worth a small fortune. One last night of pretend and she would be satisfied forever.

Only, it hadn't gone at all the way she'd planned. When she'd reached the drawing room, she'd peered in from the corridor, at first delighted to see her Mr. Whitland, only to realize he wasn't alone. He was surrounded by three beautiful young women. Of course, he was surrounded by beautiful young women.

Maddie's heart had sunk. She'd realized her mistake immediately and rushed away, only to be utterly shocked when Mr. Whitland himself followed her. And when he'd admitted that he had thought of her all year, she had been overcome with emotion. Enough to kiss him of all reckless things!

Maddie's throat closed as she stared off into the darkness

outside the small window between the beds. A memory came floating back to her. A memory of a night when she'd made the most reckless decision of her life.

THE DAY MR. LEOPOLD HERBERT came to town had been the worst day of Maddie's life. It was funny, actually, how the worst day of one's life could resemble so many of the days before it, without a hint that one's entire world was about to change forever.

As they had every morning since Papa had passed away, Maddie and Molly had awoken, dressed in their shabby yet service-able dresses, and gone about making the best of their circumstances.

Apparently, Papa hadn't made arrangements regarding where the sisters should live. He'd been counting on the fact that his cousin Harry would come and take care of both Maddie and Molly.

Only, a letter written to Cousin Harry's address had been returned with some awful news. Seemed Cousin Harry had died a few months earlier in a carriage accident. Word had never got to Papa apparently, or if it had, he'd already been too far gone with consumption to do anything about it. A distant cousin named Leopold Herbert would inherit all Papa had, including the estate and the title of Baron Atwood. Mr. Herbert would be coming from Carlisle in Cumbria, where he'd worked as a farmer for the last thirty years.

Maddie and Molly had never heard of Cousin Leopold. Papa had certainly never spoken of him. They had waited patiently for months before the man graced them with his presence. He barged into the house that afternoon, slamming the door open so forcefully it cracked the plaster on the wall behind it.

Maddie had been startled from her work in the basement where she was washing the laundry for their tiny household. There had been no money since Papa's death because it had all been entailed to Cousin Leopold.

Maddie had gone rushing up the stairs into the foyer to see what was the matter, only to find a large, dirty man striding about the rooms of her beloved home as if he owned the place. It wasn't long before Maddie realized he did own the place.

"Who are you?" she'd asked, raising her chin and eyeing him with distaste.

"I am the owner of this household. Who are ye?" he had replied in a smug tone. He was girthy and brash and wore clothing that looked as if it had not been washed in weeks, which contributed greatly to the smell that was following him from room to room. He looked to be at least fifty years of age.

"No, you're not," Maddie snapped back. "My father is..." But she'd stopped short, her breath catching in her throat. Oh, no. No. No. No. No. No. This couldn't be. Was this? Could this be...Cousin Leopold?

"What is your name, sir?" she asked instead of completing her sentence, while horror and denial filled her mind.

"What is yer *name, washer woman?" Leopold had replied. "I don't owe ye mine."*

Maddie had sucked in her breath. Washer woman, indeed.

She lifted her chin and proudly announced. "My name is Madeline Mary Eloise Atwood."

Leopold's bushy brows had shot straight up and a smile spread across his grimy face, revealing rotting teeth. "Are ye now?"

She'd lifted her chin even higher, not liking how his eyes wandered over her. "Yes," she managed to choke out.

"Where's yer sister?" he asked next, and it took everything in Maddie to keep from refusing to tell him.

"Molly is upstairs."

"But yer the eldest, ye said?" he continued, rubbing his chin and narrowing his eyes on her.

"Yes. I'm eighteen years old."

"That'll do."

Maddie fought her shudder. "What do you mean, 'that'll do'?"

He scratched his dirty head. "I mean, ye're the one o' age...so yer the one I plan ta marry."

Maddie had been forced to cup her hand over her mouth to keep from retching. "Marry?"

"Yes, indeed. Yer lucky I ain't been married afore."

Lucky? She fought her revulsion.

"I don't even know you," she said, casting about for a better argument but finding none that wouldn't be outright insulting to the odious man.

"We're ta marry in the mornin' and that's me last word on the subject," Cousin Leopold insisted.

In addition to his being rude and slovenly, Madeline did not take kindly to his orders. There was no way she would marry this man. "I shall not marry you," Madeline had countered, raising her chin, and hoping the fear making her entire body shake wasn't apparent in her voice.

"Ye ain't got no choice," Cousin Leopold replied. "Wit yer pa dead, ye and yer sister are my wards. If ye refuse to marry me, ye can both find somewhere else ta live. I'm offering ye the chance ta keep yer family name and house, ya daft girl. Ye should be on yer knees thanking me."

"I thank you for nothing," Madeline had snapped, her chin wavering. "And if the choice is marrying you or leaving, we shall leave immediately."

She'd turned on her heel and made her way up to her bedchamber in her childhood home before her knees buckled and she slid to the floor near the wall. Molly had come rushing in to hug her. Her sister's slight thirteen-year-old body shaking with tears. "I heard," Molly said. "Do you truly think it's best if we leave?"

"I won't marry him," Madeline had insisted. "Go, pack your bag."

Tears streaming down her face, Molly had complied and within the hour, they were both wearing last year's cloaks and standing near the front door. Madeline turned to take one final look at the only home she'd ever known, realizing with an aching throat that she might never see it again.

"Let's go," she'd said to Molly, taking her hand and doing her best to seem brave and confident while her knees were knocking together beneath her skirts.

They'd slept in the barn that night, snuggled together in the hay. But the anger that had filled her chest the moment Cousin Leopold had ordered her to marry him kept Maddie warm. She would do anything for her sister, anything but marry a man she didn't love.

The next day, the sisters had gone to their former housekeeper in the nearby village. Mrs. Halifax took them in out of love, but Madeline knew the poor woman and her elderly husband needed money. "I'll go to London and find work," Madeline had promised. "I'll send every farthing back here."

The next day, she'd left for London using money Mrs. Halifax had loaned her to purchase a ticket into town on the mail coach. Molly had tried not to cry but had to wipe away tears as she said good-bye.

"Don't worry, Molly. I'll be back for you. I'll be back and when it's time you'll have the future you deserve."

Molly had solemnly nodded and done her best to wipe away her tears with the handkerchief Maddie had given her.

"Be brave," she'd told her sister. "Listen to Mrs. Halifax and help her around the house. I'll write you every sennight, I promise."

It had nearly broken Maddie to leave her sister, her bright blue eyes red from crying as she'd trudged away in the snow toward the mail coach.

And just last month, Maddie had received the letter she'd been dreading all these years. "Your cousin Leopold has offered for Molly," Mrs. Halifax wrote. "It would be a fine step up in the world for the girl to become a baroness."

The worst part was...Mrs. Halifax was right. Maddie had

left four years ago, thinking she would make her fortune in London. And now, here she was, barely able to scrape by and making careless mistakes. Perhaps she *should* have married Cousin Leopold all those years ago. At least she'd be the one saddled with him now and not her poor dear Molly. It made Maddie's stomach churn to think of it. If she'd only sacrificed herself when she'd had the chance, Molly would be safe now and able to pick a husband of her choosing. Molly wasn't like Maddie. Molly craved stability and was easily frightened. She would marry him, Maddie knew, unless she found a way to get her sister out of there. But there was little chance she would ever be able to afford to give her sister everything she deserved.

Maddie shuddered again as she glanced around the small, bare room she shared with Anna. She'd failed her sister. Her wages weren't enough to buy a Season's worth of fine clothing. She could barely pay for Molly's room and board at Mrs. Halifax's house.

Maddie clenched her jaw. Her own selfishness and recklessness had caused all of this. And she'd been selfish and reckless again tonight, risking her position in the Hazeltons' house by sneaking downstairs one more time.

She was struggling to reach the buttons on the back of the pilfered gown when Anna came rushing into the room.

"I stopped by the drawing room," Anna said, a clearly disappointed look on her face. "It was empty."

"No. He was there," Maddie hastened to tell her. She turned again and motioned for Anna to help her remove the borrowed gown.

"He was there?" Anna nearly squealed as she quickly unfastened the buttons and helped Maddie step out of the pink gown.

As she pulled on her simple black maid's gown that she'd

left lying on her bed, Maddie recounted precisely what had happened on the staircase.

"You kissed him?" Anna's dark-brown eyes widened to round orbs.

"Yes." Maddie nodded happily, unable to squelch her smile at her own boldness. She had plenty to regret, but she'd never regret that moment.

Anna sighed dreamily and laced her fingers together. "Oh, what was it like?"

"It was...lovely," Maddie said wistfully. "And now both of my dreams have come true. First, I danced with a handsome gentleman at a ball and then I kissed him. Now, I'm *never* taking a chance like that again. As soon as I give back this gown, these slippers, and these earbobs—" She gasped.

She'd been reaching for the earbobs as she spoke. The left one was missing. Maddie's heart plummeted to her feet and nausea roiled in her middle.

"Anna, quickly! We must find the other earbob or I'm certain to be sacked!"

CHAPTER EIGHT

J ustin remained standing on the staircase, blinking. He'd done a thing most unlike himself. He'd chased a lady up a staircase. Why? Why had he followed her? He'd obviously gone mad. He wasn't one to brag, but usually women chased *him*. He'd never had to follow one down a back corridor and up a servants' staircase while asking her to stop before, that was for certain.

He scrubbed a hand through his hair and cursed under his breath. The other events that had just unfolded were equally nonsensical. He'd asked Madeline for her surname. She'd refused to tell him. *Again*. Then she'd *kissed* him. Fully. On the lips. And while the kiss hadn't been lengthy, and she hadn't even employed her tongue, he'd felt it to his toes. Which was also rare. It had been years since he'd been affected by a mere kiss. These days, kisses for him were merely a necessary stop on the road to lovemaking, not something that sent a jolt directly to his groin, but here he was, uncomfortably shifting in his breeches, trying to figure out why an innocent peck from a debutante had made his entire body rock-hard.

He scrunched his eyes shut, then opened them again, shaking his head. He glanced up the stairs, wondering for the second time in two years if the entire encounter with her had merely been a figment of his imagination.

It was madness. That was all. She'd said, *I do hope you have a lovely life.* That clearly indicated she never intended to see him again. The kiss notwithstanding.

The entire thing was simply...confusing. In all his years, he had never had any such encounter with a young lady. Madeline didn't want him to know her surname. She'd made that abundantly clear. It would drive him to distraction, not knowing. But how would he ever learn it?

He turned around in a tight, frustrated circle, half wondering if he shouldn't continue to chase her up the stairs and demand her name. Though he had every reason to believe she wouldn't give it to him. And he would be an ass to continue to follow a woman who had clearly said good-bye.

Blowing out a breath, he glanced down. A sparkle caught his eye. He leaned closer. A diamond earbob lay on the edge of the stair just above where he stood. He leaned down to further inspect it. It was one of the diamonds Madeline had been wearing. He was certain of it. It had obviously dropped from her ear during her flight. He leaned over and picked it up.

A smile spread across his lips. Well, now he *had* to find out who she was. Didn't he? Even if he never used the information to contact her, he would have to return this valuable piece of jewelry. A gentleman could not do otherwise. But how would he find her? He couldn't very well go upstairs and search every room.

He had to think. What did he know about her? Her name was Madeline. She was a guest. And she'd...gone upstairs. That must mean she was staying here. And given her age, no doubt Lady Henrietta knew precisely who she was. That was it. He'd begin by asking Henrietta Hazelton.

CHAPTER NINE

J ustin tucked the earbob in his coat pocket and made his way back into the ballroom. He didn't have to search long for Lady Henrietta. She had a loud laugh and wore extremely long feathers atop her head. She stood out like a partridge.

He casually made his way to the small group where she stood. The most expeditious way to do this would be to ask her to dance. It would be worth a dance with Lady Henrietta to learn who Madeline was or where he might find her. He gritted his teeth and bowed to the lady.

"May I have this dance?"

Lady Henrietta exchanged a look with her mother that could only be described as dumbfounded.

"Me?" She pointed at herself, her mouth slightly agape, her large front teeth on full display in her too-small mouth.

"Yes." He kept his most charming smile pinned to his face, even though it pained him.

"Yes!" She launched herself into his arms, propelled no small amount by a hearty shove from her mother.

Justin helped her regain her footing. Then he took her

hand and placed his other at her waist. She stepped closer to him and grabbed his shoulder. The white feathers jutting from her coiffure nearly poked out his eye.

Another waltz began to play, and in a word, the dancing was…awkward. She stepped on his feet more times than he cared to count and made a sort of snorting, honking noise by way of an apology. At least he presumed it was an apology. It may well have been an issue with her throat and nostrils. She held on to him far too tightly. She clutched at his shoulder as if she would fall without his support and her fingers in his other hand were icy and skeletal beneath her gloves. He did his best to keep the smile plastered to his face, but he wasted no time coming to the point.

"I have a question for you, Lady Henrietta," he began, wincing as she stepped on his foot again.

The lady stumbled, falling into his arms, causing him to have to right her and assist her in regaining her footing. "A question?" she croaked in a particularly braying voice that sounded exactly like a donkey.

The way she repeated 'question' while leering at him made him wish he'd used another word. For heaven's sake, she couldn't possibly think he was going to *offer* for her on the dance floor after one-quarter of an awful dance, could she? This was precisely why he detested these sorts of affairs. A lot of marital aspirations and nonsense.

"Yes," he replied stiffly, hurrying to quickly disabuse her of any misconception as to the nature of his question. "I had the pleasure of meeting one of your guests earlier tonight."

Lady Henrietta's face crumpled into a frown. "A guest?" she repeated, turning up her nose and sneering the word.

"Yes, a young lady, actually," Justin continued.

Her frown turned into a dark glare. "And?" she asked woodenly.

"She dropped an earbob, and I thought perhaps if I

showed it to you, you might recognize it. We hadn't been introduced yet, and I don't know her name."

"Very well," Lady Henrietta said with a long, loud sigh.

"Excellent. Thank you." Justin was thrilled to have a reason to end the dancing. He led Lady Henrietta to the side of the room, where he pulled the earbob from his coat pocket and presented it to her.

She glanced at it and her orange-brown eyes narrowed. At first, she looked entirely uninterested, but then she leaned in closer and glared before taking the bob from his hand and rolling it over in hers. "Where did you get this?" she hissed.

"I found it. On the floor. I believe your guest dropped it. I didn't receive a formal introduction, but I believe her Christian name was...Madeline." There. That was true. He only hoped Lady Henrietta didn't ask him how he'd managed to come by a lady's Christian name and not her surname.

Lady Henrietta's eyes narrowed to slits. "Madeline?" She dragged out the name in an overly exaggerated fashion. "Are you *certain* her name was Madeline?"

"Yes." He nodded. Damn. Had he made a mistake? It didn't appear that Henrietta knew anyone named Madeline.

Lady Henrietta pursed her lips, her eyes darting back and forth as if she was contemplating the matter. "I only know... wait. What did she *look* like, my lord?"

"Blond hair, blue eyes. Your height." He also wanted to say the most beautiful lips and startling dimples he'd ever seen and mention that she smelled like fresh lilacs, but he refrained.

Lady Henrietta's nostrils flared, and her face turned a mottled red. "I see," she snapped.

"Do you know her?" he prompted, eyeing her carefully. She certainly seemed to have *someone* in mind.

"I believe so," Lady Henrietta managed through a clenched jaw.

Hope bloomed in Justin's chest. "Who is she?" he asked a bit too quickly. "So that I may return the earbob," he added, to seem less excited to learn the news.

Lady Henrietta closed her long fingers over the earbob in her palm. Her eyes remained slits. "She is no one you would know, my lord. No one of consequence. I shall return the earbob myself." She turned on her heel and stalked away.

"Wait—" Justin called, but Henrietta had left so quickly she was already halfway across the ballroom.

Justin followed her long enough to see that she went out into the foyer and up the grand marble staircase at the front of the house. He couldn't follow her up there. Damn it. It wouldn't be proper. Now he'd not only lost the chance to learn who Madeline was, he'd lost the blasted earbob. He resisted the urge to punch the nearest wall.

Five minutes later, he found himself standing outside of the drawing room where he'd first met Madeline. He stared at the door and took a deep breath. He knew she wouldn't be there, but he couldn't help himself. He'd been inexorably drawn to the room again.

This time, when he opened the door, the room was occupied, though not by Madeline.

His sister Eliza sat on a cream-colored settee near the fireplace reading a book. Her profile was highlighted by the candle that rested on the table beside her.

Justin exhaled his breath. No doubt Mama was looking for Eliza. She tended to hide in unassuming places in order to read. Well, *he* certainly wouldn't reveal her secret. "May I come in?" he asked.

"Yes, as long as you're not chatty," she replied without looking up from her book.

"Then perhaps I should go." Justin was not at all secure in his ability to remain silent at the moment.

This time Eliza looked up and snapped shut her book.

"You're never chatty. Come sit." She patted the space next to her with a free hand.

He strolled toward her, but instead of sitting, he paced slowly in front of the icy windows behind the settee while he rubbed the back of his neck. "Have you been here since I left?"

"Yes," she admitted with a sigh. "But if you see Veronica or Jessa, please don't tell them. They'll want me to do something awful...like dance."

He chuckled. He'd always appreciated Eliza's directness. He felt much the same as she did, which made it easy for him to sympathize. "Aren't you going to ask me the identity of the young lady I was looking for?"

"Absolutely not," she replied. "I've no intention of prying into your personal affairs. I leave that for the other ladies in our family. They're adept enough at it." She gave him a sly smile.

He returned the smile. "Her name is Madeline." He told his sister because he had to tell *someone*.

"Madeline who?" Eliza set the book atop her lap and her folded hands atop the book.

"I don't know her surname." He scrubbed a hand through his hair. "All I know is that she's beautiful and blond and has the brightest blue eyes I've ever seen and dimples that could tempt a saint."

"Dimples that could...I must say, I've never heard you describe a lady like *that* before," she replied, cocking her head and blinking at him in surprise.

Nodding, he continued to pace. "Yes, and I don't know why I'm doing it now."

"I certainly know little about such things, but it sounds as if you might be smitten. Every time Jessa is smitten, she says things that sound like that."

"Blast. I'm turning into Jessa?" He used both hands to

scrub through his hair this time.

Eliza chuckled. Then she stood and hefted her book in one hand. "As I said, I'm hardly an expert, but I do promise not to tell the others."

"I know you won't," he murmured, shaking his head. "That's why I told you."

"Is that all you know about her?"

He shook his head. "I know she lost a diamond earbob. I returned it to Lady Henrietta because I didn't know Madeline's surname."

"Didn't Lady Henrietta tell you her surname?"

"No," he groaned. "She took the earbob and went upstairs."

"Upstairs?" Eliza blinked. "That is curious. Do you think she means to keep it?"

"I do not know." He stopped and braced a hand against the windowsill. He stared out into the dark night beyond the cold panes of glass. "Regardless, I'm quite certain I'll never see Madeline again."

CHAPTER TEN

The Mayfair modiste. If there was a worse place in the civilized world to spend an afternoon, Lady Elizabeth Whitmoreland didn't know where it was. Oh, she supposed torture or war would be worse in an objective sort of way, but wasn't being poked and prodded and endlessly measured its *own* sort of torture?

While she'd *never* enjoyed going to the modiste, these days it was particularly excruciating because she had an entire *wardrobe* to procure. Ballgowns and day dresses and shifts and stockings and stays and hats and reticules and ribbons. All the *accoutrements* for a young lady about to make her debut. And all a lot of silly nonsense if you asked Eliza. How many day dresses did one person need? Certainly not a round dozen, which was how many Mama had ordered for her. And those were in addition to the dresses she'd ordered for Jessa. Why, Justin's house would be overrun with day dresses. And if the day dresses seemed excessive, the number of ballgowns on order was ludicrous.

Meanwhile, Jessa flitted about the shop crooning over

ribbons and stroking silks as if her wildest dreams were coming true. Eliza steadfastly detested being fussed over. And the modiste's shop was as fussy as fussy got. Nothing made her more impatient than standing on a short wooden stool while Mama and Jessica and the modiste debated whether pink or violet was a more fetching color for a piece of trim around the bottom of a gown. First, Eliza preferred green. Not violet and certainly not pink. Green was a sensible color. Not overly romantic or fancy. The color of trees and shrubs and practical, useful things. To date, she'd only ever been allowed *one* green gown, and she was already scheming for ways to wear it every day.

Speaking of schemes, Eliza had tried a variety of them to extricate herself from the endless trips to the modiste, the most convincing—in her humble opinion—being that Jessa was her *identical* twin and couldn't they just make two of everything using Jessa as the model? Instead of being hailed as the obvious genius that it was, however, the idea had merely made Mama raise her eyebrow in that frightening manner that meant she was quite through with Eliza's mischief-making. It made Jessica blink at her sadly and say, "Oh, Eliza, don't you *want* to pick out all the lovely bits?"

She did *not*, in fact, want to pick out all the lovely bits, or *any* of the bits for that matter, but given the state of Mama's eyebrow, Eliza had resigned herself to come along. The only thing worse than being poked at was trying to dodge the question for the hundredth time when Mama asked her when she intended to choose a lady's maid for the Season.

Eliza had no intention of hiring a lady's maid. Why would she intentionally make it someone's profession to pick at her, poke at her, drape her in fabrics and jewels and yank at her hair? No, thank you. She detested having her hair up. It only served to make one's neck cold. But Mama refused to listen to such sensible arguments. Regardless, Eliza intended to stay exactly as she'd always been, *sans* lady's maid. She'd lived to the age of eighteen without a maid, and she would continue to do so. Jessa could have a maid and enjoy the experience. Eliza would prefer to find a quiet spot and read.

Which is precisely why she found herself hiding behind a row of fabric swaths when Jessica greeted Lady Henrietta Hazelton and her mother, who had apparently entered the shop.

After the niceties were exchanged, including much talk about how lovely the Hazeltons' Twelfth Night Ball the previous night had been, Lady Hazelton said, "Yes, well, after we finish here, we're off to the employment agency. Henrietta requires a new lady's maid."

"Does she?" Mama replied, obvious interest in her voice. "So does my Eliza. I've half a mind to send her with you."

Elizabeth winced and scrunched down further behind the swaths, hoping Mama didn't notice her.

"Why are you looking for a new maid, Henrietta?" Jessica asked in her bright, friendly voice.

"I had to dismiss my previous maid last night, during the party, actually," Henrietta replied, disgust in her tone.

"Really!" exclaimed Mama. "That's awful."

"What happened?" Jessica prodded.

Eliza shook her head. Leave it to Jessica to prod.

"The most egregious thing," Henrietta continued. "I discovered she'd stolen a diamond earbob from me."

"Oh, my goodness!" Jessica exclaimed.

"Yes," Henrietta continued, "and when I went to confront her, I found she'd stolen a gown and slippers too. Turns out, she sneaked down to the ball and pretended to be a guest. Can you imagine?"

"No!" came Mama's horrified voice.

"Yes," Lady Hazelton replied in an equally horrified tone. "Such a shame. She seemed like a nice young lady when we hired her." She let out a long, loud sigh. "It's so difficult to find good help."

"Yes, well, best of luck," Mama said as the two other women left the store.

"Don't let your sister hear that story," Mama said to Jessica when she thought they were alone. "She'll use it to argue with me about not hiring a maid."

Eliza had to smile at that. Her mother was perfectly correct. But she didn't wait to hear whether Mama said more. Instead, Eliza slipped away from the swaths to follow Henrietta and her mother out of the shop. The two other ladies were about to climb back into their waiting coach when Eliza stopped them.

"Oh, Henrietta," she called, clasping her white-gloved hands together in front of her.

Henrietta turned. "Yes?"

Eliza hurried toward her, tossing a glance behind her to ensure Mama and Jessica were still in the shop. "I, er, I wanted to ask…that is to say…would you mind terribly telling me…what is your maid's name?"

"My maid?" Henrietta repeated, frowning. "The one I sacked?"

"Yes." Eliza nodded, feeling like a fool, but entirely determined to see this through. "I overheard the story you told Mama and Jessica inside." She might be awkward, but she was also convinced she already knew the answer and wanted to ensure she was correct. There was no other way around it than to ask Henrietta directly.

Henrietta's eyes narrowed. Suspicion covered her long features. "Why do you want to know?"

Why, indeed? Eliza bit her lip for a moment while she thought of a plausible reason to ask such a question. "Er, I'm to hire a maid soon myself and I want to ensure I avoid the one you dismissed. She sounds positively dreadful."

Henrietta's frown disappeared. Apparently, she was satisfied with the answer. "I have no intention of giving her a reference, of course. She's a most egregious thief. Her name is Madeline Atwood."

CHAPTER ELEVEN

Justin sat on the sofa in the blue drawing room reading the morning paper while his mother perched on the settee opposite him, looking over the new calling cards for the twins that the print shop had sent for her perusal. Jessica sat straight-backed at the pianoforte, practicing her Bach for the hundredth time. Elizabeth lounged in an overstuffed chair in the corner, reading a book.

Justin paused for a moment in his own reading to glance around. He smiled to himself. It was nice to have company in the town house for a change. For some reason, his usual pursuits—the gambling and the drinking and the women—hadn't been quite as entertaining this past year. When Mama and the girls arrived, he'd welcomed their presence as a nice change of pace and surprisingly he hadn't missed the gaming hells as much as he'd expected to. Though no doubt it was only temporary. Once his sisters were married and Mama was back in the country, he would return to his usual pastimes with all due haste.

Of course, he'd understood this Season would be unlike

the others. He had a duty to perform. He was the marquess, after all. Therefore, it fell to him to ensure his sisters were introduced to Society in the proper manner. Mama would take care of all the details. All Justin need do was escort them to a ball or two, host one himself in their honor, and then field the scores of marriage offers they were certain to receive. He would choose the best man for each of his beloved sisters, taking into account their desires, of course. Then they would marry, and by this time next year, they would be out of his hair, happily installed in their own households, and he would be back to his bachelor lifestyle. Precisely what he longed for.

Oh, he would have to marry as well, eventually. But he'd managed on his own all these years, and after seeing what Edgefield had been through with Veronica, Justin wasn't in a particular hurry to tighten the parson's noose around his own neck. He would enjoy a few more years of fun, thank you very much. After all, he was his father's son.

~

"KEEP UP, BOY," Father said, as Justin attempted to spur his mount to keep pace with the larger horse.

At thirteen years of age, Justin wanted nothing more than to please his father. He rarely came to the countryside to visit Mama and his children and when he did, Justin was usually at Eton. But this was the summer holiday, and Father had come home expressly with the purpose of teaching Justin about running the estate. "You're my heir," Father said proudly each time he showed him a new bit of the property, "and all of this will be yours one day."

Justin had done his best to listen to Father and make him proud, but truthfully, he was wary of the man. Wary and not a little...disgusted. Father had a habit of coming home and making Mama cry. It had happened time and again since Justin's earliest memories. At some point he and Veronica had come to expect it. Mama and Father would shut themselves in the room down the hall from the nursery. Mama would beg her husband not to return to London and his mistress, and Father would apologize and agree. Only to leave months later to Mama's sobbing.

At first, neither Justin nor Veronica had even known what a mistress was, but as they'd grown, they'd worked it out. While Veronica had turned angry at their father, Justin had resigned himself to disgust. Justin loved his mama so fiercely, he hated to see her cry. He couldn't understand why Father would ever make her weep.

Justin had followed his father all the way to the far end of the pond that graced the middle of the property when Father stopped, dismounted, and tied his horse to a nearby tree. He waited for Justin to do the same before clapping him on the back and guiding him down toward the water's edge.

Justin sucked in his breath. He'd been waiting for a moment like this for months, years even. He was so rarely alone with his father. Today he intended to confront the older man about his abominable treatment of his wife.

"I'm glad we've had the chance to spend the day together," Father began, staring out across the still water. "I daresay it's long past time I should have begun teaching you how to go about being the marquess."

"Indeed," Justin replied, his tone sharp. He straightened his shoulders and folded his arms behind his back, summoning the nerve to say what he must. "We could spend more time together if you weren't so often in London."

Father's bellowing laughter rang across the pond. "Ah, now, you cannot blame me for that, my boy. London holds much more excitement than the country. You'll see soon enough. I intend to take you back with me."

"Pardon?" Justin's head snapped to the side to face his father.

"That's right," Father said, a wide smile on his face. "You're

nearly fourteen years of age, Justin. Your birthday is next week. It's high time I show you the pleasures London has to offer a young man of your station."

Justin swallowed hard. He wasn't at all certain he was ready for whatever pleasures his father was speaking of, but spending more time with his father and getting to see more of London—he'd only visited a time or two—was intriguing.

"I'll take you around, introduce you to some of the girls," Father continued.

"The girls?" Justin replied, his throat going dry.

"Oh, they'll love *you. Especially the younger ones." Father waggled his brows.*

Justin swallowed again. "Yes, well, I wanted to speak with you about something...else."

Father frowned. "What is it?"

"It's mother. She's terribly upset about your m-mistress." There. The word had nearly lodged in his throat, but he'd managed to get it out.

Father's face turned to a mask of stone. "Your mother shouldn't speak of such things to you."

Justin cleared his throat. He'd gone this far, he had to see it through. "On the contrary, she hasn't. It's just that I...I've over-heard your arguments and Veronica and I—"

"You and Veronica have no business listening to my private conversations," Father snapped.

Justin forced himself to lift his chin. He refused to back down. "I don't like to see Mama cry."

Father's countenance softened, and he moved closer and clapped Justin on the shoulder. "Neither do I, believe me. It's hardly my choice that she gets so emotional. But men...we have...needs...and those needs are often best fulfilled by, well, the types of ladies one encounters in London. You'll see."

"I don't want—"

"Of course you don't. Not now. You're young yet. But I

wouldn't be doing my duty to you if I didn't introduce you to the pleasures of London Society. Out here, I've taught you to sit a horse, meet with tenants, command servants, and keep the books, but in London, well, you'll see." His father gave him a leering wink.

Justin recoiled and forced himself to clear his throat and try again. "But Mama—"

"Your mother has always been far too emotional. And Veronica is just like her, I'm afraid. But you, you my dear boy," he clapped Justin on the back again, "you're just like me and you always have been."

Justin had swallowed hard, fear spreading through his chest like fire. Dear God. Was that true? Was he just like his father?

A month later, Justin arrived back at the estate after his trip the London. He rushed inside to greet Veronica, Mama, and the little twins. Veronica was out riding her horse. The twins were napping. But Mama was there. Dear, sweet Mama hugged Justin fiercely the moment he launched himself into her arms.

"How was your time in London?" she asked, a bright smile on her face.

Justin cleared his throat, not wanting to share any of the details with his mother. They were not appropriate, and Father had warned him to keep such things to himself.

"I had a fine time," he said solemnly. The truth was, he'd taken to the London scene like a duck to water. His father had been right. He was just like him. Justin had drunk too much, kissed beautiful young women, played card games, learned curse words, smoked several delightful things, none of which were good for him, and when he'd finished all that, he drank some more. He'd never had a better time.

But now that he was with his mother, guilt tugged at his conscience. He knew well the things Father did in London were the things that made Mama cry.

"I'm glad to hear it," Mama said, wistfully staring out the front window at the drive. "Did your father...stay in town?"

"Yes," Justin admitted, pushing the tip of his boot along the carpet.

Mama tried to fake a smile for him.

"Are you sad again, Mama?" he managed to ask, regardless of the lump in his throat.

She shook her head. "I'm just glad to have you back, dear."

"But you miss Father?" he prompted.

Mama stared wistfully off into the distance. "It's my own fault. I never should have married for love. It's absolute hell to give your heart into another's keeping."

JUSTIN SHOOK his head to clear it of the uncomfortable memory. For some reason, the image of the mysterious Madeline flashed through his mind. Last night he'd been prepared to rip the town—or at least Hazelton's house—apart to find her, but after a good night's rest, he'd realized he'd been foolish to think he should continue to look for her. Even if he found her, what would he say? It wasn't as though he intended to *court* her, nor as though she were the type of lady looking for an *arrangement*.

She was almost certainly a debutante, and he was *not* looking for a wife. When he did look for one, he would be looking for a lady who wanted no more than his title and her place in Society. Not one with romantic notions and the desire to dance at balls. That was the same sort of young lady who was looking to fall in love, and Justin wasn't the sort to fall in love. Just like his father, he would *not* make a good husband. And while he *was* just like his father in every other way, Justin would *not* repeat his father's mistakes. Father had married a woman who loved him and wanted him to be faithful. Justin knew better. He had no intention of putting a loving wife through hell.

It was much better that Lady Henrietta had taken the earbob and disappeared. Justin had already decided that he would not question her further on the subject. There was no sort of future for him with Madeline, no matter how captivating his two brief interactions with her had been. He was better off concentrating upon launching his sisters into Society. To that end, stubborn Eliza needed a lady's maid. Mama had discussed the matter with him in his study just this morning. She'd asked him to speak to his sister on the subject. Now was as good a time as any.

"Eliza," he said, folding down the edge of his newspaper to look at her. "I intend to call upon the employment agency tomorrow to find a proper maid for you. You may come with me if you wish, but either way, I plan to leave the appointment with a good prospect to hire."

Eliza didn't so much as lift her eyes from her book. "Oh, there's no need, brother. I already found someone."

He blinked and frowned. "You did?"

"You did?" Mama stopped her perusal of the cards. She met Justin's gaze with a mixture of amazement and disbelief on her face.

"You did?" Jessica echoed, the pianoforte falling silent.

"Yes," Eliza replied. "In fact, she's upstairs getting settled now."

"I'm happy to hear it," Mama replied. She exchanged an impressed look with Justin. If Mama wondered how Eliza had managed to locate and hire a maid so quietly, she didn't mention it.

"That's right," Eliza continued. "I received a recommendation from a…friend and settled it all yesterday."

Justin eyed his sister carefully. He didn't miss the funny little smile on her face even while her attention remained focused on her book. She was up to something, but regardless, if she'd found a maid, it was one less thing to worry about, and that suited Justin. "That's sorted then," he said, settling back in his seat and snapping open the paper once again.

"Where is the new maid?" Jessica asked, obviously pleased that her sister had given in and done the proper thing.

Elizabeth pointed a finger skyward. "I believe she's upstairs unpacking her things. I intend to go up in a few moments and show her about. I'll send her down to meet you later, Justin."

Justin didn't look up. "No need. If you like her and Mrs. Sherman approves, I'm certain I shan't find fault." His housekeeper was as discerning as they come, and he trusted her implicitly.

"Oh, I'm *certain* you'll like her," came Eliza's confident reply.

CHAPTER TWELVE

Maddie turned in a wide circle to survey her new bedchamber. It was larger than the one at the Hazeltons' residence and she'd been informed by Mrs. Sherman that she was to have this room all to herself. What a luxury! In addition to a bed that was much grander than the one she'd left, with a newly filled fluffy clean mattress and half a score of thick, freshly laundered blankets and down pillows, the room also contained a bedside table, a wardrobe, and a small writing desk. At the Hazeltons', she and Anna had been forced to share a small, rickety dresser and there hadn't been wardrobe or desk in sight.

Besides the improved facilities, when Mrs. Sherman told Maddie what her wages would be, Maddie was convinced it was a mistake. Only, she'd been too cowardly to ask in case she'd be pointing out an error that would be quickly rectified. The amount was nearly double what she'd made working for Lady Henrietta, and Maddie desperately needed it. Just this morning, she'd received a letter from Molly telling her that things were getting worse in Devon. Her sister had written to say that Mrs. Halifax had been encouraging Cousin Leopold's visits. Apparently, the dastardly man was coming by twice a week to pay a call on Molly, which meant Maddie had even less time than she'd thought. She intended to write back to Molly posthaste, provide her sister with her new address, and ask Molly to wait before making *any* rash decisions. The more time Maddie had, the better. The increase in wages here was certainly a step in the right direction. She only hoped Molly would listen.

Lady Elizabeth Whitmoreland. That was the name of the young lady Maddie was to serve now. She was certain she'd never met her or her mother, which was odd, and the way Maddie received notice of the new position was odder still. After being summarily sacked by Lady Henrietta two nights ago in the middle of the Twelfth Night Ball, she'd packed her things. The Hazeltons' housekeeper had taken pity on her and allowed her to sleep on the floor in the kitchens as long as she promised to be gone by dawn. She'd woken up with the sun, gathered her small bag with the few items she owned, and taken off into the cold, foggy morning to wait outside the employment agency.

Looking back, the only good thing that had happened the night of the ball—besides her first kiss—was the fact that Lady Henrietta had somehow found the diamond earbob. She'd also found Maddie in her room with Anna, still frantically searching. Lady Henrietta had also found her borrowed gown, slippers, fur stole, and the other earbob. Of course, it looked as if Maddie had stolen the items. There might have been a reason for her to have the slippers and gown in her room if she were mending them or cleaning them, but there was *no* good explanation for Maddie to have the earbobs. The earbobs had been her biggest mistake. They'd been so lovely and sparkly and elegant. She'd had every intention of giving them back the moment she was finished pretending.

Embarrassed and deeply ashamed, she had foolishly attempted to explain herself, which had only made the situation worse. Lady Henrietta had looked as if she might have an apoplectic fit when she'd heard that Maddie had sneaked downstairs in her ballgown and earbobs. In the end, Lady Henrietta had been convinced Maddie was both a thief and a liar, and Maddie couldn't blame her. She'd made a horrible mistake. One that she'd been certain would cost her life in London and her sister's entire future.

Maddie spent the next day at the employment agency, waiting in a long line for a chance to see Mrs. Hestrom, the proprietress, and explain herself. Mrs. Hestrom had been entirely unsympathetic and had explained that without a reference from Lady Hazelton, which she was certain to never receive, Maddie would not be able to procure another position as a lady's maid. Not in London, at least.

Maddie had been convinced her only option would be to return to the country and attempt to secure some sort of work there. It would pay far less, but what option did she have? She had been about to leave the employment office and trudge to the mail hack to secure a spot on the next coach to Devon when Anna had appeared quite unexpectedly and given her the card of a lady who had come to the back stoop of the Hazeltons' house looking for her.

The card had been from one Lady Elizabeth Whitmoreland and a note scribbled upon it asked her to come round the next morning to the servants' entrance of the Marquess of Whitmore's town house and ask for Mrs. Sherman. Maddie had barely believed her good fortune.

She'd managed to beg one more night sleeping on the floor of the Hazeltons' kitchens and then she'd arrived promptly this morning with Lady Elizabeth's card in hand. She'd been hired on the spot (no references required—thank heavens) and shown to this lovely room.

It was possible, neigh *probable*, that Lady Elizabeth would be an even more demanding and curmudgeonly employer than Lady Henrietta had been. Why else would a young lady hire a maid without an interview, or requiring a reference? No doubt, the woman had gone through maid after maid and was desperate. But that was fine with Maddie. She was desperate too. And for whatever reason, whether it was divine intervention or strange fortune, she was not about to question her blessings.

A knock on the bedchamber door startled Maddie from her thoughts. She rushed over to swing it open. There, standing in front of her, was a beautiful young lady. She had dark hair, dark eyes, lovely high cheekbones and a friendly smile on her face. She was wearing a simple but expensive-looking green gown, and her hair was down, and it looked as if it could use a good brushing.

"Good morning," the young lady said. "I am Eliza, and you must be Madeline. Thank you so much for accepting the position."

Maddie's mouth nearly gaped open. This beautiful young lady, her new mistress, was thanking *her*. And she'd introduced herself as Eliza, not Lady Elizabeth? "No, no, my lady," Maddie hastened to say. "It's I who should thank *you*."

"Nonsense," Lady Elizabeth replied, still smiling. "You've no idea how desperately my mother has been nagging me to find a maid. I do hope I'm not too much trouble. I shall endeavor to cause you the least amount of it possible. But apparently, when one has one's debut, one must do things like change into new gowns every time one turns around and have one's hair set atop one's head. A lot of nonsense if you ask me, but I suppose I cannot avoid it. Believe me, I've tried."

Maddie's smile widened. Apparently, Lady Elizabeth was unconventional. Maddie liked her at once and had to bite back several hundred questions. Such as how exactly the lady had come by Maddie's name. Best to hold her tongue for now until she had a better sense of Lady Elizabeth's character. And why court trouble by bringing up the dreadful Hazeltons?

"Come with me," Lady Elizabeth said, gesturing for Maddie to follow. "I'll show you my rooms and my things. Some gowns and bonnets are still on order at the modiste, of course, but there's already a dreadful lot of it."

Maddie smiled again at her new mistress's disgusted tone. Lady Elizabeth was not anticipating her upcoming Season with enthusiasm, to put it mildly.

Shutting the door to her bedchamber behind her, Maddie gladly followed the young woman to the servants' staircase, where they began their descent.

"I'll introduce you to Mama and Jessa, my twin sister. She's also making her debut, and she's much more interested in it than I am."

"Oh, how lovely it must be to have a twin sister," Maddie exclaimed.

"It is lovely," Lady Elizabeth replied. "Only, I haven't quite worked out how I can convince Jessa to pretend she is me half the time so I may skip all those dreadful parties for the Season."

Maddie couldn't help the laugh that flew from her lips. "I'm terribly sorry," she immediately exclaimed.

"No need to apologize," Lady Elizabeth replied, pushing open the door to the second floor and marching through it. "If you have any ideas, please do let me know."

They made their way down a corridor lined with an expensive runner, its walls graced with gorgeous oil paintings. If her own bedchamber hadn't already informed her, Maddie would have realized immediately that this family was much wealthier than the Hazeltons.

A few moments later, Lady Elizabeth stopped. "Here we are. Mine is the fourth door on the left. Jessica's is directly opposite. Let's go inside. I'll show you all the gowns. Then there's something I need you to take downstairs to my brother. I believe he's in his study."

CHAPTER THIRTEEN

J ustin scanned the daily report from his solicitor.
Years ago, he'd instructed the man to keep the thing
to one page. All Justin required was a certain set of
figures to ensure his estates were running smoothly.
Fortunately, he was quite skilled at numbers and it took him
no time to evaluate both the solicitor and the report. He
made his rounds to speak to his tenants quarterly and otherwise, he enjoyed his life in London. The less responsibility,
the better. Just as Father had taught him.

A tentative knock pulled him from his thoughts. "Come
in," he called absently, assuming it was the butler or the
housekeeper with another question about the twins that he'd
no doubt refer to his mother. What did he know about young
ladies' debuts and their endless requirements? He was quite
happy to pay the invoices that seemed to arrive on his
doorstep hourly and leave the details to Mama.

He glanced up as the door to his study opened. In
walked...*Madeline*? He blinked and shook his head. He had to
be seeing things. But when he looked again, Madeline still
appeared to be standing just inside the doorway to his study.

She had turned pale as a ghost and her mouth fell open.

She was dressed as a servant—black gown, white apron, and white cap—and she held a piece of paper in her hand.

What the devil?

He stood in a rush of confusion. "What are you doing here?" The words flew from his lips as he searched her face.

"What are *you* doing here?" came her equally shocked reply.

"This is my house." As explanations went, it barely scratched the surface, but his mind was still struggling to catch up.

"*You're* the Marquess of Whitmore?" she asked in a tone that implied she didn't believe it.

He bit his bottom lip and winced. Damn. "Yes." What else could he say?

"But you said..." Her brow was furrowed, and she looked as if she wanted to turn and run.

He closed his eyes briefly. "I said my surname was Whitland. A slight variant. It is Whitmoreland."

"You said you were a mister," she replied in a high-pitched voice that Justin found adorable even while guilt spread through him.

"Actually, I never *said* that," he replied, still biting his lip. "You assumed it and I did not correct you."

"And I..." Guilt washed over her fine features. "Didn't tell you the truth either." Her shoulders slumped, and she glanced down at the floor. "I'm a lady's maid. Your sister is Lady Elizabeth?"

Justin expelled his breath. Hands on his hips, he shook his head. It suddenly made sense. All of it. "*You're* Eliza's new lady's maid?"

Madeline nodded. "Yes. She hired me this morning after I was—"

He narrowed his eyes on her. "After you were what?"

Madeline hung her head. "After I was sacked by Lady Henrietta Hazelton."

Justin rubbed his forehead between his thumb and forefinger and stared at the ceiling. If it had all made sense a moment ago, now the entire story somehow made *perfect* sense. It made sense and it was unbelievable at the same time. Obviously, Eliza had been paying close attention during their talk at the Hazeltons' ball. She'd somehow learned Madeline was a maid, and she'd installed her directly in his house. But what was this about being sacked?

"You were Henrietta Hazelton's maid?" He asked it as a question, but he already knew the answer.

She nodded. "Yes."

"And she sacked you because...?" Nausea roiled in Justin's gut. He'd asked another question to which he feared he already knew the answer.

Madeline let out a shaky sigh before replying, "Because she found out I had borrowed her clothing and her jewelry to attend the Twelfth Night Ball."

Justin closed his eyes as more guilt washed over him. Wave after wave this time. *Bollocks. Damnation. Hell. And bollocks again.* He scrubbed a hand through his hair. "I'm sorry, Madeline. I'm afraid that is *my* fault."

"Your fault?" she repeated, the crease in her brow becoming more pronounced. "How could it possibly be your fault?"

He groaned and winced. "Because I'm the one who brought Henrietta the missing earbob and asked her if she knew anyone at the party named Madeline."

She was quiet for a few moments, obviously allowing the information to settle into her mind before she finally shook her head. "No. No. It was my fault, my lord. I shouldn't have borrowed Lady Henrietta's things. It was an outrageous thing to do. I deserved to lose my position. And I will understand if you decide to sack me on the spot. Only, I hope you will believe that I did not know this was *your* household when I came here this morning."

"I believe you," he replied. "And while I admit I'm certainly surprised to learn you're a maid," he straightened his shoulders, "I have no intention of terminating your employment. After all, I'm responsible for the fact that you lost your other position. I'm not about to toss you out."

She expelled a long sigh, which told him how relieved she was to hear his decision. With it came a dazzling smile and those tempting dimples. "Thank you, my lord. I promise I will not do anything as foolish as trying to sneak into a ball again. I am in need of this position, and I will not do *anything* to jeopardize it. You have my word."

Justin nodded, feeling like the biggest arse in the land. He'd got this poor girl sacked. He'd chased her up the staircase, made her lose her earbob, and then got her sacked. She should want nothing to do with him. The least he could do would be provide her gainful employment for as long as she needed it.

Madeline glanced down and appeared to remember the document in her hand. "Here," she said, taking long strides toward his desk to give him the paper. "Lady Elizabeth asked me to bring you this."

"Did she?" Justin asked, quirking a brow. A quick glance at the paper revealed it was nothing more than another bill from the modiste. But the fact that Eliza had sent Madeline as the courier told him something important. His sister clearly wanted him to know she'd located his missing dance partner. "Thank you," he said to Madeline.

She spun toward the door to leave, but as she was about to step into the corridor, she turned back hesitantly, one hand resting on the door handle. "It can't be a coincidence, my lord. Can it? That I am here."

"It's not," Justin admitted. "I mentioned our meeting to my sister. But not to worry. Eliza is the soul of discretion. She would never tell your secret, and neither would I. I promise not to make your work uncomfortable. Please stay."

Madeline nodded. "Thank you, my lord. I will. Though I hope we can both agree to forget about our dance." Her face flushed a charming shade of pink and her voice lowered to a whisper. "And our...k-kiss?"

"Consider it forgotten," he replied with a nod.

Relief covered Madeline's face, and she left the room, closing the door behind her.

Justin stared at the empty space she'd just left, cursing himself seven times a fool for ever mentioning Madeline's name to his meddling sister. He should have known better. All the women in his family were meddlers. Even Grandmama.

He rested his hands on his hips and poked out his cheek with his tongue. To make her feel more at ease, he'd promised Madeline he'd forget their dance and their kiss, but he had no idea how the hell he'd manage either.

CHAPTER FOURTEEN

addie left the study quickly, yet she slowed as she climbed the stairs back to Lady Elizabeth's bedchamber. She needed time to sort through her feelings. First of all, she was embarrassed. She'd never expected to see Mr. Whitland again. She'd *counted* upon not seeing him again, actually.

She certainly never would have *kissed* him if she thought she'd see him again, let alone be *employed* by him. The fact that he knew she'd been sacked by Lady Henrietta for something so silly and fanciful was embarrassing too. It was *beyond* embarrassing. Her cheeks flamed just thinking about it.

But second of all, she needed this position. Depended on it. Had no other options, in fact. So, she would have to recover from her embarrassment at once. Besides, how often would she see her mistress's brother? She'd be relegated to the fourth and second floors most of the time. She would remain abovestairs except for meals and outings. There was little chance they would encounter each other.

And thirdly, except for the fact that she'd made a

complete fool of herself to her new employer—a marquess, no less!—and *kissed* him, this position was already better than her previous one. The wages, the accommodation, and her new mistress were all far superior to life at the Hazeltons'.

She would be a fool to leave over a silly bit of embarrassment. If Lord Whitmore didn't want her gone, Maddie wasn't about to give up such a lovely place and a generous salary. He'd been nothing but kind to her and had given her no reason to believe he would be anything but kind in the future. He may have misled her about his identity when they met, but she'd misled him too.

As for her most egregious transgression, the kiss. Well, that was in the past, wasn't it? It wasn't as if she could have a future with a *marquess*. Her playacting, her fantasies were over. She was mortified that she'd been found out by the man she'd been playacting with. But that's what she got for being so selfish as to sneak downstairs and try to insert herself somewhere she didn't belong. Her one consolation was that he'd lied as well. They were even on that score.

Now, she needed to count her blessings and do her best for Lady Elizabeth. And while Maddie might very well turn pink every time she saw her new employer, she would just have to overcome that for the sake of her sister, her position, and her future. She'd been given a second chance. She'd be a fool not to take it.

She still wasn't entirely certain how Lady Elizabeth had known who she was just because her brother had mentioned the name Madeline, but did it matter? The fact was, she'd been sacked, and now she was here.

Maddie pushed open the door to Lady Elizabeth's room. The young woman was perched on a sage-green settee in front of the wide windows, reading a book. Maddie had already learned that her new mistress loved books. It was a charming trait, really. The moment Maddie stepped into the room, Lady Elizabeth pulled the book down to her nose and blinked at her. Maddie kept a blank smile pinned to her face.

"Did you meet my brother?" Lady Elizabeth ventured innocently. "He's a very nice man. I can assure you."

Maddie allowed one of her brows to lift. "I think you know I've already met your brother."

The book slid away from Lady Elizabeth's face to reveal her wince. She quickly snapped the book shut and set it on the settee while standing and biting her lip. "Guilty."

Maddie nodded. "I am quite grateful, Lady Elizabeth. Please don't misunderstand me. But I must ask: Why did you do this? Why did you hire me?"

"I hope you'll forgive me and allow me to explain." Lady Elizabeth folded her hands together. "The main reason I hired you is because I know what an awful person Lady Henrietta is. It can't have been pleasant working for her. And I was telling the truth when I said I was sorely and quickly in need of a lady's maid." She paused. "And finally, I hired you because you're the first young lady in whom Justin has taken any interest whatsoever."

Maddie clapped a hand to her throat. "Interest?" She choked. "But...I'm...I am...a lady's maid. Surely you cannot mean that your brother and I—"

Lady Elizabeth waved a hand in the air, dismissing Maddie's words entirely. "You're a lady's maid at present. I've read enough to know one's circumstances can change when one least expects." With that cryptic message, Lady Elizabeth left the room, the book still firmly in her hands.

Maddie watched her go, a riotous mass of confusion still ringing in her head. Her new mistress's last words had been correct, however. One's circumstances *could* change when one least expected. It had already happened to her.

Twice.

CHAPTER FIFTEEN

Justin remained in his study and drummed his fingers against the top of his desk. Guilt continued to pound through him. He'd got Madeline (he still didn't know her surname, blast it) terminated from her position. The poor girl had only been trying to enjoy herself at the ball for a bit. Perhaps unconventional, perhaps slightly odd, but understandable.

There was something endearing about it that made him wish she'd got away with it. She'd clearly wanted to enjoy herself and he remembered how excited she'd been to have one dance. Only, he'd come along with the earbob she'd lost and got her sacked. Still, how in the world had Eliza pieced it all together and learned that Madeline had lost her position? To that end, Justin had sent up a footman with a summons for his meddlesome sister.

It didn't take long for a tentative knock to sound at the study door.

"Come in," he intoned.

Eliza entered with a completely innocent look on her

face. She'd always been good at feigning innocence. Not as good as Jessica, but adept, nonetheless.

"You asked to see me," Eliza announced, stepping inside and closing the door behind her. Her omnipresent book was tucked under her arm.

"Take a seat." He gestured toward one of the two large leather chairs in front of his desk. It wasn't lost on him that his stubborn sister's hair was down, and she was wearing that blasted green dress she refused to take off. Both things were battles for another day, however.

She slid into the chair and sat up straight. She perched on the edge of her seat, blinking at him expectantly as if she hadn't a care in the world.

Justin shook his head. He might as well get directly to his point. Eliza wasn't one to deny guilt after she'd been caught. She was level-headed that way. "What precisely were you thinking hiring Madeline?"

"I was thinking I was saving her from Henrietta Hazelton," she replied without missing a beat. She'd obviously been prepared for this conversation. "She sacked her, you know? The night of the ball."

Justin winced. Guilt poked at his conscience again. "Yes, I know."

Eliza set her book on the desk in front of her. "When Mama and Jessa and I saw Henrietta at the modiste yesterday morning, she mentioned she'd just sacked her maid for stealing an earbob. I asked her name and the moment I realized it had to be *your* Madeline, I rushed to find her. You know how Mama's been after me to hire a maid. And everyone knows Henrietta is awful. I couldn't let the poor girl be tossed on the streets. Henrietta wasn't about to write her a reference."

So *that's* how Eliza had found out about Madeline. She'd run into Henrietta. Regardless, he couldn't argue with any of his sister's points. Instead, he insisted, "She's not *my* Madeline."

"Isn't she though?" Eliza replied, inclining her head toward him and crossing her arms over her chest.

"Certainly not."

"Oh, I'm sorry. I thought it was you who mentioned her beauty, her blue eyes, and her dimples that could tempt a saint. Perhaps that was my *other* brother." She finished with a far-too-certain-of-herself smile.

His nostrils flared. "I thought you promised not to pry into my personal affairs."

"I didn't pry. You offered that information, which was so unlike you, by the by, that I assumed you were looking for assistance. You wanted to find the girl." Eliza shrugged. "Well, I found her."

Justin rubbed his forehead with a knuckle. Damn it. He couldn't argue with Eliza's logic. He had brought this on himself, hadn't he? Would he ever learn to *never* tell his sisters things? *Any* of them? "Fine. I might have mentioned her dimples, but that doesn't make her mine."

Eliza shifted in her seat. "If that doesn't make her yours, perhaps the fact that you're the reason she was sacked does."

He groaned as if he'd been slugged in the gut. Nothing Eliza could have said would have made him feel more guilt. And she wasn't wrong. He cursed under his breath.

Eliza crossed her arms over her chest and lifted a brow. "Our family *owes* Madeline a position, Justin."

Justin leaned back in his chair and scratched his chin, cursing the entire situation for the dozenth time. "I agree, and I have every intention of allowing her to stay. But I want to make one thing clear." He deepened his voice and leaned toward his sister, doing his best to appear the ominous head of the family. "You had better not be trying to matchmake. It's beyond inappropriate for more reasons than one. No more sending Madeline on errands to my study. Do you understand me?"

"You'll let her stay?" Eliza asked, a bright smile spreading slowly across her face.

Justin expelled his breath. "I have no choice. I *am* the reason she was released from her position. I feel awful for the young woman."

"Oh, thank heavens." Eliza pressed a hand to her throat. "I was certain you'd send her away. I cannot imagine having to go on the hunt for another lady's maid."

Justin arched a brow, giving his sister a highly skeptical glare. "I don't for a second believe *that* is the reason you hired her."

"Of course it wasn't." Eliza stood, grabbed her book, and rushed back toward the door. "But if it happened to solve my problem as well, all the better."

"One more thing," Justin said, still staring directly at his younger sister.

"Yes?" she chirped, a half-smile pinned to her lips.

"Neither of us are to mention a word about Madeline's former position to Mama or Jessica or Veronica."

"Of course not. I wouldn't do that to Madeline," she agreed.

"Oh, but *I'm* fair game?" he asked, shaking his head.

"You have my word. From this moment forward, Madeline is simply my new lady's maid." And with that, his sister hurried from the room.

Justin stood and paced to the window, where he looked out over the park across the street. He was attracted to Madeline. That was simply a fact. He hadn't been able to stop thinking about her for an entire year. Also a fact. But she was a maid. *A maid.* It wasn't that he was a snob and couldn't imagine himself attracted to a maid. On the contrary, he already knew he was wildly attracted to her, and he didn't give a bloody damn about her station in life. What bothered him was the fact that he was now her *employer*. It would be beyond dissolute of him to take advantage of a woman in his employ.

Oh, he knew of noblemen who did such things, of course. But Justin had always found it exceedingly distasteful. He prided himself on being a fair and honest employer. He was responsible for Madeline now, and he refused to be the sort of man who chased after the staff in his own household. He shuddered to think of it.

He and Madeline may have shared an enjoyable interlude at a party a time or two, but that was over now. She was his sister's maid, and he would treat her with nothing but the respect due a member of his household staff. Besides, how often would he see her? He'd made it clear to Eliza that she must not send Madeline on invented errands to find him ever again. If his sister listened, everything would be fine. He took a deep breath. Very well. Problem sorted. There would be no issue whatsoever with him and Madeline living under the same roof.

CHAPTER SIXTEEN

"We're off to Lady Bainbridge's for dinner," Mama announced later that evening as Justin entered the drawing room. "Are you certain you don't want to join us?"

"And be ogled by Lady Bainbridge's shrill daughter? No, thank you. Have a pleasant time," he finished with a sweeping bow. Normally, he didn't go out 'til much later, but he was staying in this evening for reasons he did not care to explore.

"You always think every young woman is after you, Justin," Jessica said, rolling her eyes.

"That's because most of them are," Eliza pointed out.

"Well, what does he expect?" Jessa sniffed. "He's a handsome, eligible marquess."

"I suppose the only thing worse than being a debutante is being an eligible nobleman," Eliza said with a long sigh. "I do feel sorry for you, brother."

"Thank you, Eliza," he replied, bowing to his sister. "I appreciate that. Mama has never properly understood my plight."

Mama waved her hand in the air. "Nonsense. If you would simply choose a bride, you wouldn't have to worry about all of these young ladies throwing themselves at you. The answer to your problem is quite simple."

"Not nearly as simple as you make it sound," he replied as he escorted the three ladies to the front door. His finest coach waited outside.

After the door closed behind them, Justin turned to look at the empty foyer. Normally, he relished the quiet. Normally, he'd be up in his rooms at this time of night reading the afternoon paper and preparing to go out on the town for a night of…well, debauchery. But tonight? Tonight, he was restless. Tonight, he didn't relish a visit to the gaming hell.

He went back into the drawing room and sat on the edge of the sofa for a moment. Then he stood and made his way to the window and stared out across the street to the park. He turned in a circle and groaned. This was boring. He needed to go out. It was completely unlike him to stay home. What would his cronies think? It was his turn to win the fifty pounds from Edgefield.

But he already knew in his gut why he wasn't upstairs preparing for yet another night on the town. It was because *she* was here. Madeline was somewhere upstairs. And Justin couldn't shake the desire to see her. It was absurd, of course. He had no business with her. And even if he did, it's not as though he could go up to the maids' rooms in search of her. That would be inappropriate, bordering on scandalous. No. No. No. He would simply go upstairs to his bedchamber and read. Yes. That was it. When was the last time he'd enjoyed a night in simply reading? He couldn't wait to get started.

∽

Twenty minutes later, Justin found himself on the second floor of his town house casually walking toward...Eliza's bedchamber. He hadn't been on this floor in years. His bedchamber, wardrobe, and bath were on the third floor and his sisters' rooms and the rooms his mother used when she visited were all on the second floor.

What was he doing here? Oh, he'd gone up to his room and found a book, but after reading the first page again and again, he'd finally tossed it aside and decided to take a tour of the second floor. After all, he should ensure it was up to snuff. It was his sisters' lodgings as they made their debuts. The rooms should all be in proper order and repair. Not that he didn't trust his housekeeper and his butler, but one could never be too certain of things. A diligent homeowner should see to each floor upon occasion...ensure there were no problems.

As he approached the door to Eliza's bedchamber, he noted that it was slightly ajar. When he drew nearer, the sound of soft humming met his ears. It was coming from inside the room. He pushed the door wider with one booted foot and stepped inside.

Madeline stood in front of the wardrobe, bathed in the light from the candles on the nearby mantel and from two candles that sat in braces on either side of the bed. She was folding clothing and humming, a soft smile on her face.

"Working so late?" he asked in a quiet voice.

She startled and turned, but the moment she recognized him, her face softened into a smile.

"My apologies," he hastened to add. "I didn't mean to frighten you."

"I didn't expect to see anyone here," she explained. "I'm trying to become familiar with everything before the Season begins."

He slowly walked to stand a few paces away from her.

The lilac scent he remembered from their dance at the Hazeltons' lingered in the air. It reminded him of spring just around the corner. It suited her. Fresh and happy. "How long have you been a maid?" he asked, folding his arms over his chest and leaning his shoulder against the wall.

Madeline continued her folding. "Four years now. Ever since Lady Henrietta made her debut. This will be my fifth Season in London."

"Where did you live before coming to London?" he prodded.

He didn't miss that her gaze slid toward the floor, and she cleared her throat before answering. "In the country."

He narrowed his eyes. "Where?"

"Devon."

He decided to stop pursing that particular line of questioning. Obviously, she didn't care to share more about her past. For the life of him, he couldn't explain why he wanted to know so much.

"I'm sorry I got you sacked, Madeline."

She paused and turned toward him, the corners of her lips lifting in the semblance of a smile, and her dimples popped. "I'm not."

His brows shot up. "Pardon?"

She looked as if she were suppressing a laugh. "I know it's awful to admit, but it's much lovelier here and I have my own room and your sister is *so* much more agreeable than Lady Henrietta. I'm rather pleased at how it all turned out, actually. Besides missing my friend, Anna, that is."

He chuckled. He appreciated her candor. "I see. Well, then, perhaps I'm happy to have obliged?"

Madeline shrugged. "Of course, I'd prefer it if I hadn't made such a ninny of myself to my new employer, before I knew he was to *be* my new employer," she added with a self-deprecating laugh.

"Not at all," he replied, stepping closer to her again. "I am the one who should be embarrassed."

"I *kissed* you, Lord Whitmore," she reminded him. "You didn't kiss me."

He scratched behind his ear and scrunched up his nose. "Yes, as to that. If you don't mind my asking, why *did* you kiss me?"

Her face flushed that lovely shade of pink he was quickly coming to admire. "I thought we were going to forget about the dance and the kiss."

"You brought it up," he pointed out.

She groaned. "So I did. Very well, the truth is I kissed you because in addition to always wanting a dance, I'd also always wanted to kiss a handsome gentleman at a ball, and you are the most handsome gentleman I've ever seen."

For a moment, Justin thought he might blush too. He'd been around a great many women in his life, some who were quite forthright, but he'd never had someone call him handsome in such an innocent way, as if she were admitting to something she hadn't wanted to tell him. It may have been the most adorable thing he'd ever heard. The women he tended to spend time with were skilled at the art of manipulation and dissembling. Talking to Madeline was like opening a window to fresh air.

"Oh, I'm sorry," she continued, biting her lip. "I didn't mean to embarrass you and I didn't mean to be so bold that night," she continued. "But it was my only chance to..." Her voice drifted off, and she returned her attention to folding the clothing in front of her.

"To what?" he prompted.

"To make my dreams come true. First the dance, and then..."

"The kiss?" His voice was a whisper.

She blushed again and nodded.

"Yes, well. If that was your one and only kiss, I must tell you it can be much better than that."

Her head snapped to the side to face him. "Truly?"

The look of disappointment on her face made him bite his lip to keep from laughing. She seemed entirely earnest. "Yes. A peck on the lips is not much of a kiss."

She dropped the scarf she'd been folding, put her hands on her hips, and shook her head. "I suppose that's what I get for kissing you when I had no earthly idea how to go about it."

He stepped closer to her, only two paces away now, and ran the tip of his finger along the curve of her cheek. "Would you care for another chance?"

Her eyes widened and for the span of a second, he thought she would say no. But then a sly smile covered her face, and she glanced around. "Would you be so kind?"

That was all Justin needed to hear. He pulled her into his arms. A slight gasp issued from her alluring lips, and she looked up at him, her eyes sparkling pools of blue. Even as warning bells sounded in the back of his mind, he decided to take his time, show her precisely how erotic a kiss could be.

First, he rubbed his forefinger along her chin, then he moved his hands along both of her soft cheeks, pushing his fingers into the sides of her fragrant hair. He gently tipped her head to the perfect angle. Then he slowly, *oh so slowly,* lowered his mouth to hers.

At first, the brush of his lips was light, but as soon as she wrapped her arms around his neck Justin allowed his tongue to delve inside her sweet mouth.

And that's when the kiss turned ravenous. He slanted his mouth over hers and pulled her tight against his body, relishing the feel of her soft curves and the way she melted into him.

The kiss lasted minutes. Long, endless, drugging minutes.

He couldn't get enough of her. He used one hand to mold her to the length of him. The other cradled her head while he owned her mouth, until she was gasping and grasping at him. Exactly what he'd wanted.

With the last shreds of restraint he possessed, he finally pulled his mouth away and stepped back. Despite his body being on fire, he managed to say, "You kissed me the first time. Now we're even."

CHAPTER SEVENTEEN

Maddie was still reeling from Lord Whitmore's kiss while she waited for Lady Elizabeth to return from her dinner party that evening. His offer to kiss her again had been completely unexpected, but not at all unwelcome. And that's what worried her.

If Lord Whitmore was going to wander around his house at night looking handsome and giving out such kisses, she'd be lost. The man was beyond tempting. She'd told herself all day that staying here would be perfectly fine because she would rarely see him. But not only had she seen him twice today, she'd kissed him again. Well, this time he'd kissed *her*, to be precise, but did it matter? By the end, they'd certainly been kissing each other.

And what a kiss it had been. He had been completely right when he'd said that their first attempt had been inadequate. What Lord Whitmore had made her feel tonight was beyond description.

He'd said goodnight and rushed from the room immediately after the kiss. Which left her even more confused. Because when he'd said, *"Now we're even,"* she'd been about to melt like a puddle on the carpet. She'd had to reach out and brace a hand on the wardrobe to keep herself from sliding to the floor. The kiss had been...well, it had been completely unlike the first chaste kiss she'd given him at the Hazeltons' house. That kiss and the one he'd given her tonight were barely in the same family of touches.

She was still dreaming about how his hands had smoothed into her hair and how his hot tongue had played with her own when Lady Elizabeth walked into the room.

"How was your evening, milady?" Maddie asked, doing her best to banish thoughts of Lord Whitmore from her mind. She needed to concentrate on what she was here for... to be an excellent lady's maid. One who didn't get sacked. One who would receive a solid reference from her mistress someday.

"Oh, it was as boring as I expected," Lady Elizabeth announced as Maddie hurried to help her unbutton her lovely green lace gown. She'd already kicked off her matching slippers.

"Boring? How so?" Maddie asked.

"All Mama and Jessa and Lady Bainbridge wanted to talk about was *the Season*." Lady Elizabeth rolled her eyes. "Who'll be at the events of *the Season*? Who'll be hosting the events of *the Season*? Who'll become engaged by *the Season's* end? If there's anything less interesting, I don't know what it is."

Maddie was half-tempted to ask what they'd said on all of those subjects. But that would be entirely inappropriate. Not more inappropriate than kissing her employer earlier, but inappropriate just the same.

But first, there was something weighing on her. Something she had to ensure Lady Elizabeth knew. "My...my lady," she began, feeling as if she might cast up her accounts. She smoothed a hand against her stomach.

"Oh, Madeline, you know I've asked you to call me Eliza."

"No. No. I couldn't do that," she said with a shake of her head.

"I find it ridiculous that two young women so close in age must pretend to be so different, but I don't want to make you uncomfortable. How old are you?"

"I'm two and twenty, my lady."

"See. Not so far apart, we two. I'm sorry to have interrupted you. What did you want to tell me?" Lady Elizabeth asked.

"I...I wanted you to know that...I...well, I was sacked from my last position with Lady Henrietta. She sent me away without a reference that same morning you came looking for me in the afternoon."

"I know," Lady Elizabeth replied quite calmly, pulling off her gloves and handing them to Maddie. "Why do you think I came looking for you?"

Maddie's mouth fell open. "You knew?"

"Of course I knew. And as I said, I know how dreadful Henrietta is. She told me she refused to give you a reference. I had to come save you. Especially since I was aware that my brother had a fondness for you."

Maddie's cheeks flamed.

"Oh, I am sorry," Lady Elizabeth continued. "I see that mentioning it has embarrassed you. Please don't fret over it. I promised Justin. His Christian name is Justin, you know? I promised him that I would not send you on any more errands to his study. I'm sorry if that made you uncomfortable."

"No, I, er, well, he seems like a very nice man." *To kiss*, she added silently in her head.

"May I ask you a question? About your time at Henrietta's house?"

"Of course, my lady." Maddie helped Lady Elizabeth remove the emerald necklace her mother had forced her to wear.

"I'm curious. Why *did* you take Lady Henrietta's clothes and jewelry?"

Maddie's stomach dropped. The words rushed from her lips in a breathless string. "If you're concerned that I'll ever do that to you, I promise I never—"

"No. No," Lady Elizabeth hastened to add. "I'm not at all worried about *that*. Believe me, I wish I could dress you up in my gowns and send you about the events of the Season pretending to be me. I'm merely curious why you'd want to sneak into the ball."

Maddie bit her lip. "If I tell you, do I have your word you won't tell anyone. Including your brother?"

Lady Elizabeth nodded. "Absolutely."

"Very well." Maddie might as well tell her new mistress the truth. After all, Lady Elizabeth already knew the worst of it. "The truth is—in another life—I was meant to have a debut and dance with gentlemen at London balls. Perhaps share a kiss with a particularly handsome one." She paused for a moment before adding. "Oh, you must think I'm the most forward person in the world."

"Not at all," Lady Elizabeth replied quite matter-of-factly. "I've often wished that I wanted the same things other young ladies seem to want, gowns and jewels and ribbons and bonnets. I can't think of anything worse than dressing up and parading around in order to find a husband, however. And dancing is dreadfully boring."

Maddie nodded, although she disagreed. Dancing was as lovely as she'd always dreamed—kissing even lovelier—but there would be no more of either for her. Papa would be so disappointed. He'd only asked her for one thing, and she'd come perilously close to ruining everything.

She'd promised her father on his deathbed that she would take care of Molly. And she would. There was no one else left to help them. Only when she was given the most difficult choice, she'd chosen her own selfish interests over what was best for her sister. And now her sister's future was in danger. Maddie *had* to make it right.

"Madeline, did you hear me?" came Lady Elizabeth's soft voice.

"No. I'm sorry. What did you say?" She took her mistress's soft night rail from a hook in the wardrobe and helped her pull it over her head.

"Come sit," Lady Elizabeth said as soon as the night rail was settled. She lowered herself to the edge of the bed and patted the space next to her. "You seem to have a great deal on your mind."

Tentatively, Maddie moved over to the bed and took a seat next to her mistress. Henrietta had never invited her to sit and talk. Aside from Anna, Maddie had had no one to talk to these past four years.

"You said you were meant to have a debut," Lady Elizabeth said frankly. "What did you mean by that?"

Maddie took a deep breath. "If I'm to tell you, I must ask you again not to share it with anyone."

"You have my word," Lady Elizabeth replied, nodding sagely.

Maddie closed her eyes briefly. Somehow she knew her secrets would be safe with the sensible young woman. She took another deep breath. "My father was a baron," she admitted.

Lady Elizabeth's eyes widened, but she remained silent.

"He died when I was eighteen. When I refused to marry my awful cousin who inherited Papa's title, he put my younger sister and me out."

Lady Elizabeth gasped. "No." She reached over and covered Maddie's cold hand with her own warm one and squeezed it encouragingly.

Maddie swallowed. "I came to London to find work. I send every farthing back to Molly."

"Your sister?" Lady Elizabeth prodded.

"Yes."

"Oh, dear. I'm so terribly sorry." Lady Elizabeth squeezed her hand once more.

"Don't be, my lady. I made my choice. I only regret that Molly has suffered because of it. I have been terribly selfish. I love my sister dearly, and I would do anything for her. But I refuse to marry for anything less than true love."

"You seem like a very resourceful, caring young lady to me, Madeline," Lady Elizabeth said, squeezing her hand one final time before pulling hers away. "I believe your sister is extremely fortunate to have you."

Maddie stood and expelled her breath. That was kind of Lady Elizabeth to say but she knew in her heart how selfish she'd been. Meanwhile, it felt oddly freeing to have shared her secret with Lady Elizabeth. She felt better than she had in days. "If there's nothing else, my lady. I'll just be going."

"May I ask you one more question?" Lady Elizabeth said. "And I promise to tell no one the answer."

Maddie nodded. "Very well."

"You mentioned your dance. Has my brother also kissed you?" Lady Elizabeth's dark eyes flared brightly with interest.

Maddie's cheeks flamed again. She pressed her hands to them, knowing they must have turned bright red.

"Oh, I'm sorry," Lady Elizabeth added. "I'm far too blunt." She shook her head. "I shall gather from the color of your cheeks that the answer is probably yes, but I shall not push you to say it."

"Thank you," Maddie breathed, only too relieved to be spared from admitting the truth to Lord Whitmore's own sister.

"There is one thing you should know about Justin, however," Lady Elizabeth continued.

"What's that?"

"I'm told my brother is a 'rake,' whatever that means."

CHAPTER EIGHTEEN

Justin spent the better part of the morning just as he'd spent the remainder of the previous night…cursing himself. He wasn't only a fool. He was a scoundrel. He was Madeline's employer, for Christ's sake. What in the world was he doing taking liberties with her in his sister's bedchamber? He'd kissed her and then he'd fled like a coward. After tossing back several whiskeys that did nothing to relieve his guilt, he'd finally gone to bed where he'd tossed and turned until falling into a fitful slumber.

The few hours of sleep did little to improve his self-directed temper. He couldn't delude himself that he'd gone to the second floor for any other reason than to find Madeline.

After telling himself all day yesterday that he would stay far away from her—that he would allow her to go about her duties as Eliza's maid without any interference from him—he'd sought her out at the first opportunity. And then *kissed* her, of all dastardly things.

He may have expressed sincere regret for the part he'd played in the loss of her previous position, but now he owed her another apology. The worst part was, he didn't even regret it.

Not truly. He felt guilt, he wasn't a monster, but that kiss had been like nothing he'd ever experienced. From the second he'd touched her, pure lust had shot through his body. Her innocent responsiveness made his blood pound unmercifully. Her encouraging smile. The way she bit her lip. He had been close to losing control. Too close. He'd wanted nothing more than to keep going. Move his hand down to her breast, pull up her skirts, toss her onto the bed and cover her with his rock-hard body. He wanted to do it again even now, mired in guilt and regret.

He was an unmitigated arse, taking advantage of his sister's maid. She may have felt guilty for being sacked by Henrietta Hazelton for sneaking around and pretending to be a guest, but she'd never lied to him. He'd been the one to make assumptions about who she was. She'd never claimed to be a debutante.

What sort of libertine was he? If his mother knew what he'd done, she'd kick him out of his own house. And he'd deserve it. Perhaps he should go? He could bunk at Edgefield's house or at his club. Only, he'd be forced to explain such a decision to his family and what the hell would he say? That he'd had to flee his own home because of an overwhelming attraction to his sister's lady's maid?

He was worse than a rutting stag. He needed a woman. It had been too long. Tonight, he would visit his favorite gaming hell and go home with a willing lady. That would solve his problem.

HOURS LATER, for the second night in a row, Justin found himself wandering through his empty house. Mama and the twins had gone to the theater with Veronica and Edgefield. Justin would be going out, but not 'til much later. But although he was home alone, he had no intention of repeating the mistakes of last night. He would *not* go to the second floor. His error last night had been giving into that moment of insanity. As long as he stayed on the first and third floors, where he belonged, he would be safe and so would Madeline. It was quite simple, really.

He would just have a drink in his study before dressing for the evening. As he made his way down the winding marble staircase to the first floor, he heard the pianoforte? He frowned. Was Jessica home? No. He'd watched her leave not an hour earlier. And Eliza never played the instrument.

Instead of going to his study, he made his way to the drawing room and pushed opened the door. There, sitting on the black wooden bench in front of the large pianoforte, was Madeline. Her graceful fingers flew over the keys as she expertly played a haunting melody. Her name flew from his lips.

Her fingers came off the keys, and she swiveled to face him, gasping.

"I didn't mean to frighten you," he said, moving farther into the room.

She jumped up from the bench and stood in front of the instrument, apprehension in her eyes. "I'm sorry, my lord. I didn't think anyone was home. Lady Elizabeth invited me to make use of the instrument while the family was out."

"*Tu joues magnifiquement,*" he said.

"*Vous êtes trop gentil,*" she replied in flawless French without skipping a beat, before clearing her throat and saying, "I...I thought you'd gone with your family to the theater tonight."

"I decided not to attend."

She gathered her skirts and made to move past him. "I'm sorry. I shouldn't be here. I'll just—"

"Please don't stop playing on my account," he said, gesturing toward the bench.

She shook her head. "It's not proper."

He chuckled. "I believe you and I left proper behind a long time ago." He nodded toward the pianoforte. "Please play. It was beautiful."

Tentatively, she moved back toward the bench and sat down. After a few moments, she resumed playing.

Justin wandered over to the instrument and braced an arm atop it. "Tell me something. How did you learn to play so well?"

Her fingers shifted on the keys and an awful noise emitted forth. She laughed and started again. "I…my mother taught me." Her voice was unnaturally high and there was a bit of a squeak to it.

"I see. And your speech? It's quite refined for a lady's maid. Not to mention your French."

Madeline kept her eyes on the keys. "Also my mother. I…I was raised in a…proper household, my lord."

He narrowed his eyes on her. "Exactly how proper was your household?"

She swallowed. "I…I nearly married once."

His brows shot up. "Did you?" It was not an answer, of course, but apparently it was all she was willing to give.

"Yes. I had the chance, but I…didn't take it." She finished her tune and turned around on the bench.

"I want to apologize."

"You don't owe me any more apologies, my lord."

"Yes, I do. This time I must apologize for taking a liberty with you last night."

The hint of a smile curled her lips. "As you said, my lord, we're even."

"Please, call me Justin. At least when we're alone. It feels wrong for you to call me by my title after we've kissed…twice."

She laughed at that. "I did hear that you're a rake."

He nearly choked. "Is that so? Who told you that?"

"Your sister," Madeline offered.

Justin's brows shot up. "Eliza? I should hope she doesn't know what that word means."

"She doesn't," Madeline assured him.

"Good!" He grinned at her. "So, tell me. If you had a chance to marry, why didn't you take it?"

She was a silent a few moments before saying, "Because it wasn't for love."

Justin narrowed his eyes at her. "You want to marry for love?"

She nodded firmly. "Love and only love. Not that it matters now. That time is long-since past. I've no plans to marry. I'm only concerned about my sister's prospects. I would do anything for Molly."

"Your sister?" He frowned. What could her sister's prospects be? "Is she a maid too?"

Madeline shook her head. "No, she's not."

"Where is she then?"

"She's in the country. Back in Devon. She's staying with a family friend for the time being. I used to live there too. After Papa died and we—" She cleared her throat. "Our fortunes changed."

Justin nodded. Perhaps her father had been a gambler or a spendthrift. If he'd died and left them penniless, they would be forced to rely on the kindness of friends. An unfortunate position to be in, but one he'd seen all too often among the gentry.

"I came to London to work. To send money back to Molly," Madeline continued.

He nodded again. Just as he'd suspected. "That's awfully good of you."

"After refusing my one and only proposal, I had no choice," she replied. "I've only done what I had to do, and it's not good of me at all because I put my position at risk by being so selfish."

He frowned. "Selfish?"

"Yes, exceedingly so. It was selfish of me to pretend to be a debutante for one night...or two. I knew if Lady Henrietta found out, she'd assume I'd stolen her things and sack me. Yet I still did it. I wasn't thinking of my sister that night. I was only thinking of myself."

Justin came around to sit on the bench next to Madeline, facing the opposite direction. "You're exceedingly hard on yourself, you know that?"

She shook her head and turned to face him. "That's kind of you to say. But let me ask you something, Lord Whitmore. If your sister found me wearing her clothing and pretending to be a guest at your party, wouldn't you sack me?"

Justin chuckled. "I don't think Eliza would allow me to."

"That's only because she knows what I've done and she's a bit...forgive me saying so, but she's...unconventional."

She'd made him laugh again. "I'm certain Eliza would take that as a compliment."

Madeline smiled too. "I think you're right."

"Your point is well taken, however. Though speaking of unconventional, I don't think I've ever known a maid to sneak into a party wearing borrowed clothing."

Madeline nodded. "I simply wanted to know how it felt. Just once. For one night." She had a dreamy look in her eye.

He leaned closer to her, breathing in the soft fragrance of lilacs. "And was it everything you hoped for?" he whispered.

Her cheeks turned that adorable shade of pink again. "Yes." She nodded. "Only, in my dreams, my gown is lavender, I am holding lilacs in my arms, and afterwards the gentleman I love invites me out on the balcony where he proposes marriage because he cannot live without me." She shook her head and chuckled. "Of course, that is simply being fanciful."

"It's not so bad to be fanciful," Justin replied softly. He wanted to kiss her again. Desperately so. Damn. Damn. Damn. He'd had such noble intentions, but a few minutes in her presence turned them to ashes. It took most of his strength to break the contact of their gazes, and it took his remaining strength to hastily stand and dust his hands across his breeches.

When he was several paces away from temptation, he shook his head and cleared his throat. "I must be off," he announced.

"Oh," she said. "You're leaving?"

Was he imagining the disappointment on her face? Or was it wishful thinking?

He turned on his heel so seeing her wouldn't tempt him further. "Yes, I'm going out…to the club. I…er…feel free to stay and play the pianoforte as long as you wish. Indeed, you're welcome to play it whenever you like."

He strode from the room, vowing not to look back. The sight of her sitting on the bench looking vulnerable and gorgeous would be too much. He needed to go out. Had to do it, in fact. He could not spend his evenings talking to a maid in his employ, wanting to kiss her…wanting to do much more. It was madness. Complete and utter madness. No good could come from it. Not only was she a maid, which meant she was strictly off limits to him, but she was a maid who had just informed him she wanted to marry for love. Which meant even if she was a countess, she was inappropriate for him. Love would play no role whatsoever in his future marriage.

He was exactly what Eliza had called him, a rake. He was his father's son. And what did rakes do? They went to clubs. They visited gaming hells and brothels. They charmed beautiful women and made love to them. Which was precisely what he was going to do this evening. He took the steps up to his room two at a time, trying to put as much distance between himself and the ungodly temptation of Madeline. After talking to her, sitting so close to her, breathing in her sweet lilac scent, he was hard. And there was one way to purge himself of that particular discomfort. He was going *out*.

CHAPTER NINETEEN

Maddie was the epitome of efficiency the next day. She'd pressed and organized all of Lady Elizabeth's clothing. She had put away all the deliveries from the modiste in order—by color—in the wardrobe. She'd ensured the wardrobe was swept and dusted and smelling of fresh lemon wax.

She'd even taken the liberty of picking out the two most beautiful gowns to discuss with Lady Elizabeth when she returned. Her mistress would have to choose one for the ball the night of her debut. That night was nearly two months away, but it would be here before they knew it. Such events had a way of sneaking up on a young lady.

Maddie had spent the early morning writing a letter to her sister. In it, she told Molly all about her wonderful new position in Lord Whitmore's household. Of course, she'd left out the part where she'd been sacked and had somehow managed to kiss her new employer twice. But that was hardly something she intended to share with her younger sister. Molly worried about her, and Maddie didn't want to add to the worries. Besides, she told the truth in her letter.

She *had* procured a new position in a much better household for a significant increase in wages. It was the exact sort of thing that her sister would be happy to read.

Maddie's thoughts slipped to Lord Whitmore—Justin—only when she allowed them to. First, she'd spent a considerable amount of time admonishing herself for being a fool last night. Even with Lady Elizabeth's permission, she shouldn't have played the pianoforte. She was a maid, not a member of the family. But then she'd heard Lady Jessica playing earlier in the day, and the temptation to know if she still recalled how proved too great. It had been so long since Mama had taught her, but her fingers remembered everything, and it had been wonderful.

When Lord Whitmore had walked into the room and asked her where she learned to play, she'd nearly shot to the ceiling in surprise. She'd barely been in her new position for a day before taking an unnecessary risk again. Anyone else might have sacked her on the spot, or at least reprimanded her. Justin had only encouraged her to keep playing.

Then she'd been a complete ninny, boring him with the stories about her sister and her life before she'd come to London. And she'd all but accused him of being a rake. Of course, she'd heard it *from his own sister*, which seemed quite a reliable source, but it didn't negate the fact that it had been extremely ill-mannered of her to mention it at all.

And then he'd left—both her presence and the house. Of course, he had. That's what rakes did. He was probably out carousing with friends at some den of inequity or other, drinking and entertaining women of ill repute. Maddie didn't know precisely what *that* might entail, but she knew it involved more than kissing.

That's what had her so miserable this morning. It was also why she'd thrown herself into her work. Every time she thought about Justin kissing another woman, her stomach plummeted to her slippers and melancholy spread through her.

It wasn't as if she could hope to capture the favor of a *marquess,* for heaven's sake. She was well aware of her present station in life. But it still made her exceedingly sad to think of him with someone else. Perhaps living in this lovely house and in such proximity to him hadn't been the best idea after all. Not if it was going to make her unhappy every time he went out for the evening. And from what the other servants said, it was a nightly occurrence.

Had Justin been with a woman last night? That's what a rake did, didn't he? He hadn't brought one home, had he? No. Not with his mother and sisters in residence.

But still. Maddie couldn't help but remember their kiss and how it had made her feel—hot, melty, and delicious. It made her miserable to think of him doing that with someone else.

She whirled around. There had to be something else in this blasted bedchamber to fold, hang, or clean.

LATER THAT NIGHT, after Maddie had seen Lady Elizabeth off with her sister and mother for yet another pre-Season dinner party, she lay on her bed staring at the ceiling. A book that Lady Elizabeth had encouraged her to borrow lay abandoned on her nightstand. She'd tried to read it, but every time she started, an image of Justin's handsome face, just before he'd kissed her, loomed in her memory. His hooded eyes. His long dark eyelashes. His firmly molded lips.

She got up and paced around the room. She should go down to the kitchens and make friends with some of the other maids. Not having a roommate was nice in some ways, but it was lonely here without Anna. Yes, that was it. She would go downstairs, but she would not stop on the first floor. She would go directly to the basement, to the kitchens. After all, she had made a vow. She'd vowed to stay away from him. Promised herself she would *not* go looking for him. She would keep off the main floor unless Lady Elizabeth needed her there.

Maddie began her descent to the kitchens, but somehow, the moment she made it to the first-floor landing, she was entirely unable to stop her feet from taking her directly to the door of his study.

She lingered outside the room, arguing with herself about whether she should peek inside. He probably wasn't even there. The door was slightly ajar. She only had to push it a bit to open it. She stepped inside and caught her breath.

She'd been wrong. Justin *was* there. He stood by the window, a drink in hand, staring out into the dark night behind his imposing desk. He turned quickly once he realized she had entered the room.

"Madeline," he breathed.

Her only response was a nod.

"What are you doing here?"

Why was she here, indeed? She'd better think of something quickly. "I wanted to thank you." The words flew from her lips before she had a chance to examine them.

"Thank me?" His brow furrowed. "For what?"

"For not sending me away when you found me playing the pianoforte last night."

"Of course. No need to mention it."

Was it her imagination, or did he look uneasy? Uncomfortable? As if he wanted to rush past her from the room? Even sensing all of that, instead of leaving, she shut the door behind her and boldly stepped forward toward his desk.

He watched her advance with a mixture of trepidation and curiosity in his eyes.

When she reached the desk, she glanced at the contents atop it. There wasn't much there. Lord Whitmore was quite tidy. She picked up a small smooth stone that sat atop a neatly stacked pile of papers. She turned the stone over and over in her hands, trying to determine what to say next.

"That was my father's," he finally offered.

"The stone?" she asked, hefting it in her hand and offering it to him.

He took it, and the slight brush of his fingers against her palm sent warmth through her entire body. "Yes. He found it on his first outing with my mother. They went on a picnic to the park. Mama kept it until he died. Now I use it as a paperweight."

Maddie blinked at him. Well, that was unexpected and terribly romantic. "Were your parents very in love?" she ventured.

His reply was a mixture of a snort and a cynical laugh. "Hardly."

She frowned. "They *weren't* in love?"

"My mother was," he replied, a note of regret in his voice. "My father never understood the meaning of the word."

"I'm sorry to hear that." She trailed a finger along the top of the stack of papers, keeping her eyes downcast. "My parents loved each other very much. Before Mama died, that is."

"You mentioned your father died too," Justin replied. "You and your sister are alone?"

She dared a glance up at him to find him regarding her with a tenderness in his eyes. "Yes, it's just the two of us now. That's why Molly is so important to me. She's the only family I have left." She swallowed and turned away from him, desperately trying to think of something to say to change the subject. The last thing she wanted was for him to feel pity for her. "How was your outing last night?" Her voice squeaked. She turned back to face him.

He lifted a brow.

She self-consciously crossed her arms over her middle. "I'm sorry. I shouldn't have asked that."

"No, it's fine. I did go out," he offered.

"And did you...?" She cleared her throat. She couldn't ask him if he'd found a woman to keep him company. That would be beyond inappropriate. "Did you...enjoy yourself?" she asked instead, tucking a bit of hair behind her ear.

He set his glass on the desk, then walked around it and stood directly in front of her. "No," he said. He scrubbed a hand through his hair and groaned.

She frowned. "What's wrong?"

"I'm trying to decide whether I should tell you the truth or whether I should leave this room right now."

"The truth, if you please," she said, prompted by an invisible devil on her shoulder.

He leaned down and braced his knuckles atop the desk on either side of her hips.

Maddie's breathing hitched, and warmth fizzed through her body down to her toes. She tipped up her chin. Their lips were scant inches apart. "I thought you were a rake?" she breathed.

He reached down and traced the line of her chin. "Do you know what that word means?"

She swallowed but forced herself to match his gaze. "I've half an idea. Why don't you explain the rest to me? What exactly does a rake do?" She could hardly believe her own audacity, but his lovely, dangerous words echoed in her head, making her daring and bold.

A lazy smile quirked the side of his lips. "I can't tell you that." His eyes were lazily hooded. His lips were so inviting.

"Why not?" she persisted, still staring at his mouth.

"Secret code of rakes?" Her heart hammered so rapidly it hurt.

He caressed her cheek with the back of one hand and Maddie thought she would go up in flames.

"It would be entirely inappropriate," he whispered.

Her gaze didn't falter. Excitement unfurled between her legs. She was playing this risky game and she would see it through. "I thought you knew I liked inappropriate things."

He moved his head to the side of hers and whispered in her ear. "Do you?"

Her breath caught in her throat. She was about to melt into a puddle on the floor. "If you can't tell me, show me."

$$\sim$$

JUSTIN WAS GOING TO DIE. That was all there was to it. This woman was going to kill him. With her plump lips and entrancing blue eyes, she was an alluring combination of innocent beauty and bold temptress. She had no idea what she was offering him. But he knew he wanted it. He wanted her. He wanted to pull the pins and cap from her hair and run his fingers through the luxurious length of it. He wanted to kiss her throat and touch her until she was calling his name.

By God, she was an unholy temptation. And she'd come to him tonight. He had been strong. After going out last night and attempting to find a woman to suit his needs, he'd left the hell in disgust not an hour after he'd arrived. All the women there had done nothing but bore him. They seemed overly made up and far too jaded. A pair of cornflower blue eyes and the most alluring dimples he'd ever seen had haunted him until he'd been forced to take his leave from the dark-haired beauty he'd set his sights on.

How in the name of all that was holy was he expected to

be strong if Madeline came looking for him in his study? He'd thought he'd be safe here. He hadn't been in Eliza's room or even the drawing room. He'd kept to himself, precisely as he'd vowed he would. But Madeline had pushed open the door and stepped inside as if delivering herself to him. He wanted to send her away. But then she'd started talking and now she was asking him to show her what a rake did, and he was only a bloody human after all, a mere mortal trying his damnedest to resist temptation. But when the temptation looked and sounded like Madeline, how could he possibly be expected to resist?

"A rake might do this." He leaned over her. Her backside pushed up against the desk, and she grabbed the underside with both hands and leaned into him.

"And?" she prompted.

He closed his eyes. She was going to be his undoing. He knew it. Yet he still couldn't stop himself.

He leaned down and brushed his lips lightly—so lightly—against hers. "He might do that," he whispered.

"What else?" she begged, her eyes heavy-lidded with what he recognized as lust.

"If he were *really* bad, he would do something like this." With one fell swoop of his arm, he sent everything atop his desk flying to the floor, then he picked her up and sat her atop it, pushing her back so she had to wrap her arms around his neck to keep from falling backward. He pushed up her skirts, impelled her knees apart with one leg, and stepped between them.

She gasped, clutching at his shoulders. Her wet lips parted and she was panting. The sound raked across his lower abdomen, making him rock-hard.

"Why? Wh-why would he do that?" she asked, her head tipped back, staring deeply into his eyes.

She was a siren, and he was helpless to stop his advance

on her. He let his hands roam down her sides before pulling her hips tight against his. They both groaned. Her head fell back, leaving her throat exposed to his lips. He kissed her jaw before trailing his mouth down to the delectable spot just above her collarbone where he licked and nipped at her lilac-scented skin.

His mouth came back up to her ear. "Because he would want to convince her to let him touch her."

"And what if she said yes? What if she said...*touch me?*"

Those two words were all Justin needed to hear. He grabbed her skirts and pulled them up to the tops of her thighs. His mouth swooped down to capture hers. He couldn't just kiss her, he soon found out. Because the moment his lips touched her and her head fell back and she made a little moaning sound in the back of her throat, he was lost. She still clung to his neck, unable to let go as he had her leveraged at an angle over the desktop.

His hand moved up to push away her shift and caress her warm hip. He closed his eyes and let his senses guide him as his finger found the wet warmth of her. Touching her soft, intimate skin made him shudder. He clenched his jaw.

She shuddered too. "My lord," she whispered against his lips.

"Justin," he growled into her ear. "My name is Justin."

He slid one finger inside of her and she cried out. Then he moved his finger, crooking it slightly forward to touch the spot that would make her wild. He shouldn't do this. He shouldn't have taken it this far. But he couldn't help it. There was no going back now. He intended to give her pleasure she'd never known before. He found it, that textured surface, and pressed his finger against it.

"What are you—? Oh, God," she moaned. She wrapped her arms more fiercely around his neck and clung to him, her breath shooting out in hot burst after burst.

He knew precisely what he was doing. He pressed his finger home again and rubbed her. Her breath hitched in her throat. "Oh my God, oh my God, oh my God," she breathed. He covered her mouth with his just as she let out a keening cry.

He held her as her body shook and when her breathing finally returned to rights, he pulled her back to a sitting position on the desk and turned to adjust his clothing while giving her a moment of privacy to adjust her own.

Breathing heavily, he pressed his forehead to hers. "That is what a rake would do."

CHAPTER TWENTY

Ten minutes later, Justin was back in his bedchamber, splashing cold water from the washbasin over his face. He briefly considered upending the basin and pouring the contents over his idiotic head. He glared at himself in the looking glass. He'd never wanted to punch himself in the bloody throat more than he did right now. Every word he could think of to castigate himself for his behavior flew through his mind—he was an ass, a wastrel, a profligate, a scoundrel, a cur—none of them were strong enough.

He'd crossed so far over the line he couldn't even see the line any longer. Even though he wanted Madeline with the fiery passion of a thousand burning suns, nothing could come of it. He *knew* that. He'd reminded himself of it often enough. He wasn't a child or an imbecile. He *must* leave her the hell alone. And leaving her alone meant no talking to her and certainly *no touching* her.

Damn it.

Even if he could marry a maid, he wouldn't want to hurt her. He was the son of a liar and cheater. His *father's* son.

Madeline had made it clear that she wanted to marry for love. *Love* for Christ's sake. He scowled at himself in the mirror, self-loathing pouring through his veins. Bloody hell. This was it. There were only two choices here. He could send Madeline away, give her a reference, and wish her the best. Or he could be a man and keep his bloody hands off her. She didn't deserve to lose her position because he was a rutting scoundrel. And Eliza didn't deserve to lose her maid (the only maid she'd ever wanted) simply because her brother was no better than an animal. No. No matter how difficult it was. No matter how much he wanted to break his pact. He *would* find the strength to avoid her at all costs.

From this moment forward.

MADDIE RUSHED UP to her room and slammed the door behind her. Breathing heavily, she leaned back against the wood and slowly slid to the floor. She was shaken. Shaken by how badly she'd wanted Justin. Shaken by the things he'd done to her. The things he'd made her feel, things she'd never felt before. If he had merely said the word, she would have gone to bed with him, given herself to him.

Two days ago, Maddie had been nothing but thrilled with her new position. But now she wondered if it was simply a different kind of torture. She might not have Lady Henrietta's snide comments and exacting demands to deal with, but she would be forced to be in the house with a man who drove her wild. A man she *knew* drove her wild because he'd demonstrated it on more than one occasion.

She pushed herself up from the floor and paced between the door and the far wall. *Think. Think*! She could leave here and try to find a position elsewhere. Perhaps Lady Elizabeth would take pity on her and give her a reference. But then she'd be doing Lady Elizabeth a disservice. The lady had made it clear she needed a maid for the Season and wanted one who perfectly understood how little she cared about having a maid in the first place. Maddie owed it to Lady Elizabeth to stay. At least for the Season.

All right. Very well. Maddie expelled a deep breath. There was only one other choice: stay but ensure she had no further interaction with Justin. Or at least as little as possible, which meant no more late-night talks and certainly no kissing. No touching! No seeking him out and no remaining in his presence if they found themselves alone together in a room.

Yes. That was it. They couldn't keep their hands off each other, so the answer was clearly to stay out of each other's presence. She would *not* think about him. She would *not* ask about him and she certainly would *not* go looking for him. She would stay in Lady Elizabeth's rooms, or her own bedchamber, and she would go downstairs only if she were escorting her mistress on an outing or going to the kitchens for meals. Yes. That would work. *It had to work.*

Maddie nodded firmly. It was a good plan, and one that she had to stick with no matter what. No good could come of any further interactions with Justin—No, not Justin—*Lord Whitmore*. She could not call him Justin any longer, no matter what he said. If she had any hope of keeping this position, she could not make any more mistakes.

Beginning immediately.

CHAPTER TWENTY-ONE

London, Two Months Later, The Marquess of Whitmore's Town House

Justin couldn't stand still. He paced in front of the windows inside the drawing room. Days earlier, Eliza and Jessa had made their debuts at the Queen's court. They'd attended the Cranberrys' Season-opening ball that same evening, and Jessa at least had a half a score of callers the next morning.

Eliza had been discovered hiding in the Cranberrys' library reading. Mama was already at her wits' end attempting to convince Eliza to show some interest—*any interest*—in the gentlemen to whom she'd been introduced. Instead, she'd managed to neatly avoid all of them.

Eliza wasn't the only Whitmoreland sibling who'd managed to avoid someone. Justin had done a splendid job of staying away from Madeline. In the last two months, he'd seen her only a handful times, almost always when she was on the way out of the house with his sisters. He'd steadfastly avoided eye contact. They'd done little more than politely nod at one another ever since that night two months ago, that night when he would have given his eyeteeth to take her to his bedchamber and make love to her for hours. Thank Christ that hadn't happened.

It wasn't that he no longer thought of her. On the contrary, he'd taken himself in hand more than once in the ensuing weeks, remembering exactly how much he'd wanted her that night, the way her soft skin had felt under his fingertips, the way she'd moaned and—No. That was not helping. He was busy tonight. He'd made an important decision. He couldn't think of Madeline.

Tonight, he and Mama were hosting a ball at his town house in Jessa's and Eliza's honor. Mama believed it might be the only way they could keep Eliza from the library. In their own house, they could lock the doors. Footmen were also stationed along Eliza's route to her bedchamber in case she attempted to sneak out and retreat to her rooms. Mama was taking no chances this evening.

"Oh, this is so exciting!" Jessa exclaimed as she twirled in a circle in front of the pianoforte. She wore a light pink gown and had pink flowers twined in her dark hair. She looked absolutely lovely.

Eliza sat on the settee, a thoroughly disgruntled look on her face. "It's not in the least exciting," she moaned. Eliza was wearing a light-blue gown that Mama had somehow talked her into, and while her hair wasn't nearly as elaborately decorated as Jessa's, she'd at least allowed Madeline to put it up in a fetching chignon.

"I do hope the Duke of Thornbury comes tonight. He didn't send his regrets, did he, Mama?" Jessa asked.

According to Jessica, the Duke of Thornbury was *the* most eligible bachelor (other than Justin himself) in the *ton*, which was precisely why his sister had set her sights on him. Furthermore, he was rumored to be looking for a wife this year, which made him the equivalent of a bleeding fox hunted by hounds as far as Justin was concerned. The problem was that Jessica had yet to *meet* Thornbury. He hadn't appeared at any of the balls or parties so far. But the Season was young, and Jessa was ever hopeful.

"Thornbury didn't send his regrets, darling, but neither did he send his acceptance," Mama replied. "Ill-mannered of him, if you ask me."

"Oh, Mama, don't say that," Jessica exclaimed. "He's to be my future husband. You must begin well with him."

"Seems to me that he should be worried about beginning well with Mama," Eliza pointed out. "Besides, how can you possibly want to marry someone you've never even met?"

"I've never met him, true," Jessa allowed, lifting her nose in the air. "But according to Lady Ashley Binghamton, he is every bit as handsome as the rumors would have it. Mama has already confirmed he has a large fortune, and his family line is impeccable."

"Oh, is *that* all there is to marriage?" Eliza said, rolling her eyes.

Jessica sighed and twirled again. "Lady Ashley says he's tall, and dark, and his shoulders are broad and—"

"That will be quite enough," Mama interjected, sharing a worried glance with Justin.

"I don't know what I'll do if he doesn't come to our party," Jessica continued, a pouty look on her face.

"You'll be just fine and have a dozen other suitors at your beck and call," Eliza said.

That pronouncement made Jessa smile again. "Who would you like me to introduce you to, Eliza?" Jessica asked in a singsong voice.

"Absolutely no one," Eliza returned stoically, her nose buried in her latest book.

"Now, Elizabeth Hortense Rolleston Whitmoreland, you

know I insist that you dance with at least *three* eligible gentlemen this evening," Mama declared, fanning herself rapidly.

Eliza's face remained blank. "Three is too many."

"No doubt you think one is too many," Jessa replied, shaking her head.

"It is," Eliza agreed.

This time, Jessica rolled her eyes. "She's hopeless, Mama. I swear."

Mama gave Eliza a condemning look that clearly indicated she would brook no more foolishness tonight before turning her attention back to Justin. "Can you think of anything we've forgotten?"

"No," he replied, but he continued to pace. "Everything should be in order for a delightful evening. But there's something I'd like to announce before the ball begins."

All three of the ladies stopped what they were doing, their heads snapping to face him.

Justin cleared his throat. He'd thought about this long and hard. He'd come to his final decision within the past few days, and he was set on it.

"Yes?" Mama prompted, moving to the edge of the settee, a slightly worried look on her face.

Justin cleared his throat. If he announced it to his mother and sisters, it would be real. And if it were real, there would be no taking it back. And he'd spent too many nights tossing and turning over it to take it back. "I've decided to choose a wife this Season. It's time."

If Mama wasn't the model of propriety, she might have squealed. Justin was certain he'd heard some sort of high-pitched joyful noise emit from behind her perfectly closed lips, but she merely smoothed her skirts and cleared her own throat. "Truly?" she asked in a calm, steadfast manner.

"Truly?" Jessa echoed, her eyes wide and her voice filled with a mix of excitement and skepticism.

"Truly?" Eliza intoned, crossing her arms over her chest. Her tone was pure skepticism, and she gave her brother a wary look that indicated she didn't believe him for one moment.

"Yes. I've made my decision, and it is final."

THREE HOURS LATER, the Whitmoreland ballroom was filled with guests. Eliza had managed to dance with two gentlemen (even if one of them was Justin). Jessica had danced with no less than a dozen gentlemen and was holding court with most of them near the refreshment table. As Eliza had predicted, Jessa appeared to be thoroughly enjoying herself, even though the elusive Thornbury had yet to arrive.

In an effort to be a good host and begin his search for a wife in earnest, Justin had danced with half a score of ladies, though he continued to do his utmost to elude Henrietta Hazelton, who stalked him like a lioness hunting a gazelle in the wilds of Africa.

Mama, it seemed, had wasted no time in spreading the news of Justin's intentions to every mother in the ballroom in possession of an eligible daughter. As a result, he'd found himself the recipient of a great many longing glances, purposeful stares, and tittering laughs.

He smoothed his hand down his black evening coat and straightened his shoulders. No matter. He could handle the ladies' interest. He'd been doing it most of his adult life already. Besides, he'd made his decision, and he intended to stick with it. He'd told Mama on purpose, knowing there would be no turning back once Mama informed the masses that he was intent on finding a bride. And it *was* time. High time. He was thirty years of age, for heaven's sake.

He didn't allow himself to think about the *other* reason for his decision. The one he didn't like to admit to himself, though he could not in good conscience deny. The more he had been unable to stop thinking about Madeline over the past weeks, the more he'd decided it was time to take a wife. Even though he'd managed to successfully avoid her for two long months, a wife in the house would be a strong deterrent —one he desperately needed. Even a wife who didn't care if he had dalliances wouldn't take kindly to her husband showing favor to a maid under her own roof. Yes. Taking a wife was prudent for more than one reason.

Of course, he hadn't changed his mind about what sort of wife he wanted. He'd merely changed his mind about the timing of the thing. A wife who felt absolutely nothing for him. That was the key. There were scores of ladies here looking for just such a husband. Handsome, eligible, rich. He supposed he had those qualities in spades.

Just as Jessa had pointed out about Thornbury earlier, those were the sorts of things a young woman of good breeding wanted in a husband. Love had little to do with it. Jessa hadn't mentioned love, had she? She hadn't even *met* Thornbury. It would no doubt be a simple task to find the perfect wife. All he had to do was to locate a woman from a good family with a history of breeding successfully. If she was pleasant and beautiful as well, then all the better. How difficult could that possibly be?

Only, he hadn't quite expected that his pronouncement would turn the mood in the ballroom tonight into one in which his every move was watched. He felt as if the enormous ballroom and its female occupants were closing in on him. He needed to get away. He needed to be alone and collect his thoughts.

He waited until the guests were distracted by the arrival of lemon tarts and chocolate cakes brought in on large silver platters by a team of footmen, before he turned and strode from the ballroom. He'd timed it perfectly. Desserts often served to distract ladies.

Once in the corridor, he made his way to the front drawing room. On his way, the musicians in the ballroom began to play the same waltz he and Madeline had danced to at the Hazeltons'.

He pushed open the door to the drawing room and stepped inside.

And that's when he saw her.

Madeline stood in the center of the room dancing the waltz with an imaginary partner. A smile lifted the edge of his lips. He watched silently, waiting for her to turn and see him. The moment she did, she immediately stopped short.

"Don't let me keep you from it," he said, the smile still pinned to his face. "I know how much you like to dance."

She shook her head and made to walk around him, but his arm shot out and he pulled her into his arms. "Very well then, we'll just have to dance together."

Justin knew it was wrong. He knew no good could come from it, but he couldn't stop himself from tugging her against him and breathing in her lilac scent. She smelled heavenly, just like he'd remembered in his dreams these past two months.

Tonight, she wasn't wearing a ballgown. She was wearing her black maid's uniform with a white apron. But she was still incomparable—more beautiful than any of the other ladies in the ballroom steps away.

He spun her around and around to the tune of the waltz, the strains of which were coming from the ballroom. And when the song was done, he bowed to her just as he would have to any partner. "Thank you for the dance."

"My pleasure, my lord," she replied with a curtsy. "I must go." She lifted her skirts and stepped around him.

"How have you been?" he asked, unable to stop himself.

Let her go.

She stopped short but didn't turn to face him. "I've been... I am well, my lord."

"I'm pleased to hear that." Not particularly charming, but he'd lost his head the moment he saw her.

She continued toward the door while Justin turned to face the far wall, his jaw clenched to keep from calling her back.

The door cracked open. Just one more moment. Just one moment more and she'd be gone, and she'd be safe again. Safe from the unholy urge he had to take her in his arms, to kiss her, to touch her, to—

"I heard you're looking for a wife, my lord."

Justin closed his eyes and swallowed. So close. Damn it. He'd tried. "Seems such news travels quickly...throughout the *entire* house."

"I promise I wasn't gossiping with the other servants," she said. "I simply overheard some of them talking downstairs."

"It's fine, Madeline," he replied. He turned toward her and the vulnerable look on her face nearly broke him. "I understand how news travels in a household as large as this one. If I didn't want it to get out, I shouldn't have told my mother directly ahead of a ball."

"So, it's true?" Was it his imagination or had her voice wavered?

A muscle ticked in his jaw. Why was it so difficult to say the word to her. "Yes," he finally managed. "It's true."

She left the door ajar and walked back to him. He clenched his fists, willing himself *not* to reach out and touch her. He *would* not. He *could* not.

"I hope you find someone perfect," she said softly.

If she hadn't reached out and touched his bare hand, he *might* have been able to remain strong. If her eyes hadn't looked like liquid pools of blue, he *might* have been able to keep the ache from his throat. If a hint of sadness hadn't sounded in her voice, it was *possible* that he would have been able to walk past her, out the door and back to the ballroom to continue his search for his future marchioness. But those things, combined with the fact that he'd just spent the last three hours thinking of no other woman but her, made him reach out and trace the soft line of her cheek.

She closed her eyes and trembled at his touch. The moment he heard her sigh, it was too late. *Damn it.* He'd *tried* to stay away, done his best, but tonight his control snapped. He hadn't touched another woman in all these weeks. There was something wrong with him. He knew that. He was weak. He was mad. He was *lost.* Justin pulled Madeline into his arms and his lips came down to meld with hers.

Her head tipped back, and her lips parted while his hands came up to cup her soft cheeks. He kissed her, deep and long. His tongue delved into her mouth again and again as she melded her body to his and wrapped her arms around his neck. She moaned, and he went rock-hard. His arm moved down to her lower back to pull her into sharp contact with his hardness. Her hands moved up to push through his hair, hold her face to his as the kiss deepened. And it felt so right.

Many moments later, he finally pulled his mouth from hers. Their sharp breaths mingled in the space between them as Justin pressed his forehead to hers, his hands still cupping her cheeks.

"I tried to stay away from you, damn it," he growled through clenched teeth.

"I've tried too," she admitted, her breathing ragged.

He closed his eyes and moved his hands down to cup her

shoulders. "The truth is...the truth is, Madeline, you're the only woman I can think about."

The noise that emitted from her throat was half groan, half cry as her arms wrapped around his neck once more and they continued their ravaging kiss.

Moments later, he pulled himself away from her once more. "I must return to the ballroom. My absence will be noticed tonight."

"Of course." She took a deliberate step back. Her fingertips went to her lips. "You're the host."

He closed his eyes briefly and clenched his fists again. This was agony. Pure torture. "Madeline, I—"

"Just go," she said. Her voice hitched.

Justin nodded and made for the door. What more was there to say? They couldn't keep their hands off one another. What was he supposed to do? Hide in one room of his bloody house forever? Order her to stay off the ground floor? It was madness.

When he got to the door, it was shut. An uneasy feeling shot through him. Hadn't Madeline left it open a crack? He quickly stepped out into the corridor and looked both ways. Empty, thank God. He strode back toward the ballroom, smoothing his hair and cravat as he went. One thought repeated itself over and over in his head as he went.

He was in *such* trouble.

CHAPTER TWENTY-TWO

Maddie sat on the edge of her bed, staring at the lone candle that lit the room. Ever since her latest kiss with Justin hours earlier in the drawing room, she'd been unable to stop thinking about it. She searched her mind, but she could find no reason to stop. She wanted him. He wanted her. It was that simple. Why shouldn't they spend the night together? They'd already gone too far as it was. They'd done their best to stay away from each other the past two months, and it had been a truly honorable feat. But the first time they'd been alone together in a room, they couldn't keep their hands off each other.

She'd missed him these past two months. Time and time again, she'd been sorely tempted to go in search of him. To look for him in his study, to reenact that night when he'd made her body sing with delicious pleasure. He'd said the same to her tonight…that he couldn't stop thinking about her. Perhaps if they got it over with, spent the night together, they could both move on and be normal in each other's presence.

He was planning on choosing a wife. That would change

everything. It was one thing to kiss a bachelor, but she would never, could never, dally with a married man.

Besides, it might be her only chance for a night of passion. She had no intention of marrying and it wasn't as if she planned to take other lovers. She wanted something to remember in her old age. If she spent the night with Justin, she had every indication she would remember it *forever*.

She'd never had such a reaction to another man, and she doubted she would again. More reason to take the chance. It *was* selfish and it *could* endanger her job. *Or* it might just satisfy an urge that simply needed to be satisfied and afterward they would stop this madness. There was only one way to find out. Regardless, she couldn't resist him any longer and she didn't want to.

It was settled. She would go downstairs to Justin's bedchamber.

~

WEARING NOTHING BUT A DRESSING GOWN, Justin paced near his bed. It was two o'clock in the morning. He'd said good night to all of his guests, had a drink in his study, and come up here to brood. What in the bloody hell was he going to do about Madeline?

He was no closer to coming to a decision when the door cracked open and Madeline herself slipped into the room.

Justin closed his eyes. Bloody hell. Was the universe testing him? Torturing him?

She closed the door behind her, and he was unable to speak as she moved toward him slowly, pulling the pins from her hair. When she arrived in front of him, she shook her head and cascading waves of blond fell in a tempting mass over her shoulders.

Justin took a deep breath. He wasn't about to ask her

what she was doing here. It was far past time for questions... or regrets.

Without saying a word, he scooped her into his arms and took her to the bed. She pushed herself up on her knees and pulled her gown over her head. Her stays and shift quickly followed and within moments, Madeline was naked on his bed.

"My God, I've imagined you here a thousand times," he breathed, shedding his dressing gown and joining her.

She scanned his body with her gaze while he perused hers. She was absolute perfection, all lush curves and full breasts, voluptuous hips, and long legs. The reality exceeded his wildest expectations.

She remained on her knees, and he came to meet her on his. She touched his chest tentatively, her fingers softly caressing his heated skin like butterfly wings.

He closed his eyes and groaned as her fingers moved down his abdomen to brush against his groin. But when she wrapped a fist around his hard cock, his hand shot down to capture hers.

"You cannot do that yet, Love, or this will be over far too quickly."

A sly smile curved her full lips.

He lowered his mouth to hers and kissed her deeply, allowing his hands to push into her thick hair. He cradled her head and fit her lips to his. Then he slowly lowered her to the bed.

Still kissing her, he gently pushed her on her back and covered her with his body. He twined his fingers through hers and pulled her hands down to rest on both sides of her hips. He pressed the backs of her hands into the bed, holding her captive there while he moved down her body to position his face between her luscious long legs.

MADDIE SWALLOWED. She had no clue what he was doing, but she didn't want him to stop. Delightful darts of pleasure zipped through her entire body, and she was certain she would melt.

He nuzzled between her legs, and her eyes flew wide. Surely, he didn't intend to—

"Spread your legs," he demanded.

She did as she was told, molten heat pouring through her veins. She sucked in her breath and held it.

He took one single lick. Just one, and her entire body shuddered. She closed her eyes and let her head fall back listless against the pillows. Oh, God. Why had she waited so long for this? She'd been a fool.

"I've wanted a taste of you for so long, Madeline," he growled against her quivering thigh. "I need another."

"Yes," she breathed, spreading her legs even wider for him.

He licked her again, this time more deeply. She arched her back and moaned, straining against his hands, which still held hers in place. When he pulled her delicate nub into his mouth and sucked, her breath caught in her throat and her trembling knees clamped against his head. "Oh, God, Justin," she sobbed.

He licked her until she was a quivering mass and then, when she couldn't take a moment more, he let go of one of her hands and slid his finger inside her. He found the perfect spot and pressed against her as her keening cries gave him the smuggest of smiles.

Letting go of her other hand, he rolled onto his back, panting and staring at the ceiling.

Maddie took a few moments to allow her breathing to

settle back to rights. Then she rolled toward him and pressed the length of her body to his side.

She allowed her hand to skim down his flat abdomen, relishing every inch and the way his smooth skin jumped in response to her touch.

"We can stop now, you know?" he offered, cracking open one eyelid to look at her.

"Why would we want to do that?" was her husky reply. "We're not through yet, are we?"

"No," he breathed, leaning up and shaking his head. "Not by half."

"Show me. Show me what you want," she whispered into his ear as her hand closed around his length.

JUSTIN'S COCK was so hard it was painful. And when her delicate fingers closed around him, he couldn't stop his groan. He sucked in his breath through clenched teeth and moved his own hand down to cover hers, showing her how to stroke him.

She quickly took to it like a master.

"Jesus," he breathed.

"Like this?" she asked as she squeezed him, running her cupped fingers up and down his aching length.

"God, yes. And, like this." He took her hand and pulled it up and down his length, setting a torturous rhythm.

She continued to stroke him while his hips silently pushed against her sweet palm. It was agony. He was going to come. And he couldn't come on her hand. Bad form, that.

But she didn't let go and soon he was wild, not caring as she stroked him again and again as he groaned and panted. Finally, he forced himself to pull her hand away.

"What? Why did you do that?" she asked, her eyes wide.

He pushed up on one elbow and pulled her toward him, kissing her deeply and shuddering. "Madeline, when I come, I want to be deep inside of you."

JUSTIN ROLLED off the bed and went to his bedside table where he pulled out something and arranged it between his legs.

"A French letter," he explained. "To prevent a child."

Madeline nodded and smiled. Thank goodness there was something for that. Her breath was coming so hard, it was painful. Justin returned to the bed, gently pushed her onto her back, and covered her again with his rugged body. She closed her eyes and luxuriated in the feel of the weight of him atop her. It felt so right. She wrapped her arms around his muscular neck and breathed in the scent of sandalwood under his jaw. His knee pushed her legs apart, and she felt him, hard and probing. She spread herself wider to accommodate him.

"Madeline," he breathed into her ear. "Are you a virgin?"

"Don't stop," she whispered into her ear. It was a demand, not a request.

IT WASN'T the answer he was looking for, but Justin wasn't certain he could have stopped if he'd wanted to, and he certainly didn't want to. His cock found the place it sought, and he pushed inside slowly, giving her time to adjust to the feel of him.

When he was finally seated to the hilt, his jaw clenched, sweat beading on his brow, he opened his eyes and gazed at Madeline's beautiful face. Her eyes were closed, and her

135

breathing was erratic, but she had a definite smile on her lips.

"Are you…all right?" he asked.

"I'm perfect," she replied, lunging upward, moving against his cock, making his entire body shudder. By God, if he didn't get to it, this woman was going to make him come.

He grabbed her hands and twined his fingers through them again, pressing her hands into the bedding on either side of her head. He pushed himself up and groaned as his length slid inside of her. "Jesus," he breathed as he pulled back the first time and slid in again.

Her chest rose and fell with each stroke, her head moved back and forth fitfully against the pillow. He could push into her again and again and again, and have the most intense orgasm of his life, but he wanted to make it good for her, one more time.

He pulled one of his hands from hers and moved it down between her legs to touch the nub at the center of her pleasure. Her free hand moved to his shoulder, clutching him, her fingertips digging into his skin as her heels bore into the mattress.

He smiled smugly again as he recognized the look of pure delightful agony on her face. If he kept up the steady pace of the tiny little circles he was making against her, she would come again. And that was *exactly* what he wanted.

He stopped stroking into her, intent on ensuring he pushed her over the edge first. Sweat beaded on her brow and she whimpered, her hips arching against his hand as he kept up his relentless movement again and again. Her breathing quickened, and she strained against the hand that he still held captive by her ear, her jaw tightly clenched. When he could tell she was on the brink of ecstasy, he lowered his lips to hers and kissed her to capture her pleasure cries in his mouth.

The moment her breathing slowed, Justin captured her other hand again and stroked into her, relentlessly following the unholy ache in his bollocks, knowing that the moment he let himself go, it would be the most intense feeling he'd had in his life.

He pumped into her again and again and finally squeezed both of her hands and pressed his head into the bedclothes near her ear to bury his powerful groans in the pillows.

When it was over, he rolled off her but pulled her into his arms and cradled her head in the nook beneath his chin. He fell asleep that way, stroking her hair...and knowing full well he was never going to be the same.

WHEN THE FIRST streak of sunlight hit the curtains in Justin's room, Maddie's eyes flew open. She sat up straight in bed and stretched, but she knew she didn't have long to linger. The maids would be coming soon to stoke the fire in the large fireplace opposite Justin's opulent bed. She had to go immediately.

Slipping from the covers, she collected her clothing, ensuring she had every single piece. She quickly dressed and then made her way to his side. She stood next to the bed, watching him silently for a moment. He was even more gorgeous naked with his dark hair rumpled, a night's growth of beard on his jaw. She smiled to herself, remembering all the delightful things the man had done to her body. Oh, she'd remember last night for the rest of her life, even if she lived to be *ancient*.

He turned in his sleep and hugged a pillow. She leaned down and kissed his rough cheek, allowing her fingers to run through his hair one last time. She'd never touch him again. But oh, how she had touched him last night. She leaned down and placed a chaste kiss on his rough cheek before turning and leaving the room through the adjoining bedchamber door. It would be less obvious to leave that way if any servants were about. She didn't allow herself to think that this bedchamber would be where his future marchioness would soon sleep. Instead, she cracked open the door to the hallway and peeked out. When she was satisfied that no one was there, she hurried out, down the empty corridor, through the far door at the back end of the hallway and up the servants' staircase. She made it safely into her room in mere moments.

She leaned back against the door and smiled to herself. She'd done it. She'd spent the night with Lord Justin Whitmoreland, the most beautiful man she'd ever seen, and she didn't have a single regret.

CHAPTER TWENTY-THREE

J ustin woke the next morning to sunlight streaming through the curtains of his bedchamber. Blast it. His valet should have ensured those were closed after he — Wait. No. Last night had been unlike most other nights. He hadn't come home from a club inebriated. He'd gone to bed earlier than normal. He'd hosted a ball, and he'd *spent the night with Madeline.*

He quickly rolled over to find the bed was empty save him. He pushed himself up on his elbows. She'd gone. Where? When? Was she already in his sister's rooms, waking Eliza and helping her dress for breakfast? Damn it. He pushed the pillows up behind his back, punching at them for good measure. What the hell had he allowed himself to do last night? He hadn't even been drinking...not heavily, at least. And neither had Madeline. He was certain of that. No. They'd both made the fully conscious decision to spend the night together.

They hadn't said a word. Somehow, they'd both just known it was time...it was right...it was inevitable. He wanted her. She wanted him. It was that simple. And with her arriving in his bedchamber, it had been easy. Too easy.

Damn it. He was a complete reprobate. And—a bright red spot on the white sheets caught his eye, and he glanced down to see *blood*. *Oh, my God*. He'd suspected it, but that confirmed it. She *had* been a virgin, for Christ's sake. He wasn't a reprobate. He wasn't a scoundrel. He was an utter rogue. A villain.

Justin searched the room. First, he'd had to dispose of the sheets himself. He refused to have maids gossiping where Madeline could hear. At least he'd taken precautions to ensure she would not grow heavy with child. He'd been sane enough to make that decision. But still, he had to make this right. He *had* to do something to set it all straight. This was his fault. He was the one who'd wandered into the drawing room, insisted she dance with him. He was the one who couldn't stop himself from touching her. He had no control. He could not trust himself where she was concerned. Madeline was not safe in the same house as him. That was all there was to it.

A knock sounded at his bedchamber door, surprising him. "Just a moment," he called, not about to allow any servant into the room until he'd properly disposed of the remnants of his night with Madeline.

He slid out of bed, grabbed his dressing gown from the floor, and wrapped it around himself. Then he stalked to the door and flung it open, *wanting* whichever servant was there to see that he was alone in the room.

"My lord," intoned his butler, who held a silver salver in front of him.

"Antony," he replied, nodding at the man.

"This message arrived for you early this morning. The footman who brought it asked for it to be given to you at the first opportunity."

Justin frowned. That was odd. What sort of missive was that important? "Thank you, Antony." Justin took the folded, waxed note from the salver.

He closed the door and made his way back to the bed, where he sat on the edge and pulled open the wax with his finger.

His eyes quickly scanned the short missive.

Lord Whitmore,

Please pay me a call at your first opportunity. I need to speak with you regarding a subject I believe you'll find of great interest. Her name is Madeline.

Yours,
Lady Henrietta Hazelton

CHAPTER TWENTY-FOUR

That morning, Maddie went about her chores with a determined verve. Lady Elizabeth wasn't one to chatter the way Henrietta Hazelton did. Lady Elizabeth preferred silence, actually. Or at least she was quite comfortable with it. Maddie helped her mistress dress for breakfast and then an outing with her mama and sister without saying more than a handful of words. Which, unfortunately, provided Maddie with more time than she would have liked to remember her night in bed with Justin. Flashes of his mouth on different places on her body kept making her cheeks heat, and she had to constantly remind herself to return her attention to the tasks at hand.

If dear Lady Elizabeth suspected anything about Maddie's behavior, she didn't say a word. And if she saw the heat brighten Maddie's cheeks from time to time, she didn't mention it.

"Did the Duke of Thornbury arrive last night?" Maddie finally forced herself to ask in an effort to halt her errant thoughts. She'd heard the many stories of Lady Jessica wanting to meet her true love.

Lady Elizabeth sighed. "I'm afraid not. Though it's not as if Jessa was hurting for male company."

"Did you dance with the three required gentlemen?" Maddie asked next.

"Yes, if you count my two dances with Justin. He came to my rescue."

An inexplicable lump formed in Maddie's throat. That sounded like Justin, helping his sister in her time of need. Of course he'd danced with Elizabeth. He had a knack for appearing just when a lady needed a dance partner.

But why did a mention of Justin cause an ache in Maddie's throat? It made no sense. She'd done what she'd planned. She'd spent the night with him. It has been lovely, more than lovely, actually. Unforgettable. But now it was over, and she needed to concentrate on her work. She had exorcised Lord Whitmore from her system.

Hadn't she?

Oh, blast. Tears sprang to her eyes, but she steadfastly blinked them away.

It wasn't until after Maddie had seen her charge off for the day that she allowed herself to retreat to her bedchamber and cry. And she didn't cry because she regretted what had happened last night. On the contrary, she'd enjoyed it immensely. She cried because she realized that instead of banishing Justin from her thoughts once and for all as she'd expected, she'd gone and fallen in love with him. Hearing the story of how kind he was to his sister had made her realize it.

How stupid could she be? At first, she'd only thought he was handsome. But then he'd been so kind to her, giving her a position in his household and allowing her to stay despite knowing what she'd done. Telling her she could play the pianoforte whenever she liked. And then last night, when he'd danced with her again, well, it was just too much. She was only human. And now she'd given herself to him. She didn't regret it. She'd do it again, but all it had done was make her want him even more. Make her regret that she couldn't have him. Justin Whitmoreland was thoughtful and kind and handsome. And she loved him.

An utterly hopeless state.

CHAPTER TWENTY-FIVE

J ustin's jaw was tightly clenched as he waited in Lord Hazelton's drawing room. He didn't care for being summoned, and he specifically didn't care for being summoned by Henrietta Hazelton, of all obnoxious people. He suspected she'd somehow learned (probably through servants' gossip) that Madeline was employed by his sister, and Henrietta intended to warn him that Madeline was a thief.

He already knew what he would *like* to say. It was none of Henrietta's damn business and he'd employ whomever he wished at his home. Only, that's not what he *would* say, because he'd already made a decision this morning about Madeline. They were no longer safe in each other's company. She would have to go elsewhere to live. He would personally ensure she received a glowing reference, and he would provide her with all of her wages through the end of the month, plus more to ensure she was properly housed until she secured a new position. In fact, he would find her a new position himself. Yes. That's precisely what he would do.

When Henrietta informed him of Madeline's past, he would simply thank her for her noble intentions and tell her that he intended to find his sister a new lady's maid at his earliest opportunity...which was true. And he didn't give a bloody damn what Eliza had to say about it.

When the door to the drawing room opened and Lady Henrietta entered, Justin immediately stood. Stood and then frowned when she closed the door behind her, leaving just the two of them alone in the room. She knew as well as he did that as an unmarried female, she required a chaperone for their meeting.

"Where is your mother?" he blurted, not particularly caring if he sounded rude.

Henrietta made her way to the light-blue upholstered chair directly across from him and took a seat. He waited for her to settle in before resuming his own seat.

"I didn't tell Mother you were here," Henrietta said.

"Won't the butler tell her?" He narrowed his eyes at her.

"Not if he's wise. I gave him a pound note to watch the door and keep quiet. You'll forgive me for not serving tea, won't you, my lord?" She gave him a tight smile.

Justin shifted uncomfortably in his seat. What precisely was going on here? "Lady Henrietta, if you've asked me here to tell me that Madeline was once your lady's maid, I already know."

Surprisingly, Henrietta laughed. "Oh, that's sweet. I wondered if you'd already tried to guess why I asked you here."

Justin frowned. "That's *not* why you asked me here?"

With a cunning smile on her face that Justin did not care for, Lady Henrietta leaned forward and slowly shook her head. "Not at all."

"Then why—?"

"I asked you here," she snapped, her voice becoming commanding and decidedly tinged with anger, "to offer you a proposition."

An uneasy feeling roiled in Justin's gut. What was she about? "A proposition?" he echoed.

"Yes, everyone at the party last night heard that you are planning to take a bride this Season."

Justin scratched at his jaw, still not entirely certain what game she was trying to play. "It's true, but—"

"I wasn't finished, *my lord*." Her voice had grown darker and angrier.

He eyed her carefully. "Very well, do finish," he replied tightly.

She folded her hands politely in her lap. "My proposition is that you take me to wife."

Justin had to turn his laugh into a faked cough, as Lady Henrietta was staring daggers at him and obviously quite serious. "You? *My* wife?" he repeated, skepticism dripping from his voice.

"Oh, I'm not stupid, my lord. I know you have never given me a second glance. I'm not beautiful, after all. I know that. But what I lack in beauty I make up for in cunning."

Justin furrowed his brow. He was just about done humoring this woman. She'd obviously gone mad. "How so?" he asked, wanting to be finished with this and quit the room.

"If you don't take me as your wife, I will ensure the entire *ton* knows that I saw you kissing your sister's lady's maid in the drawing room of your town house last night."

His mouth snapped shut. A muscle ticked in his jaw.

"Have I rendered you silent, my lord?" Henrietta prodded.

Justin clenched and unclenched his fist on the arm of the chair while carefully choosing his next words. He ensured he sounded as nonchalant and unaffected as possible as he said them. "You plan to ruin the reputation of a lady's maid," he scoffed. "Why bother?"

Lady Henrietta arched a brow. "That is where you are wrong, my lord."

"Wrong about what?" he barked impatiently.

"About her being a lady's maid."

"She's *not* a lady's maid?" Justin said, crossing his arms over his chest and glaring at Henrietta as if she'd lost her mind.

"At *present*, she is a lady's maid," Henrietta replied calmly. "But I happen to know something about her that you do not."

Justin's nostrils flared, but the daft woman had managed to gain his attention. "What's that?"

"Madeline comes from the Quality. Her father was a baron. The family fell on hard times, and she was forced to take a job as my lady's maid. If anyone finds out that she's not only a thief but also a whore, no one will allow her younger sister into Society, and I happen to know that is Madeline's greatest wish."

Justin swallowed. Goddamn it. His skin went clammy with loathing and disgust. Henrietta was completely vile, but it all made sense now. The stories Madeline had told. The fact that she was cultured and could play the pianoforte and spoke French. The mention she'd made of her sister's prospects. It made him sick to his stomach, but Henrietta was telling the truth. She *could* destroy Madeline's family, and Madeline's greatest concern *was* her sister. And it was *his* fault that Henrietta Hazelton held this power against them both right now.

Of course he had a score of questions about who Madeline really was and what precisely had happened to her family. But if Madeline hadn't trusted him enough to confide in him, then he certainly didn't want to hear it from Henrietta Hazelton. He also didn't relish confirming to Henrietta that she knew more about Madeline than he did.

Henrietta blinked at him and gave him another tight smile. "Now, when shall our engagement announcement appear in the *Times*?"

CHAPTER TWENTY-SIX

J ustin tossed back his third brandy of the hour and immediately ordered another one from the footman hovering near his shoulder at the club. He'd ruined Madeline's life. His ridiculous inability to keep his hands off the woman had ruined her life. Or would have ruined it if he hadn't agreed to Henrietta's plot.

He'd agreed for two reasons, actually. One, he refused to be the reason why Madeline's life was made any more difficult. He'd already done enough damage to her. Two, he had already planned to marry a woman of the Quality whom he didn't love. Henrietta wasn't beautiful, and she certainly wasn't pleasant, but that was the price he would have to pay to save Madeline's and her sister's reputations. Otherwise, Henrietta met all his requirements for a wife and, frankly, she might just make the best wife of all. Love would be nowhere near their match. In fact, he would take special delight in continuing his profligate ways with Henrietta at home.

Either way, he was still determined in what he needed to do for Madeline. There was only one thing *to* do. He would find her a new position in town, an even better position than being Eliza's maid.

Only one thought haunted him. Madeline was of the Quality. A baron's daughter. And that meant... He grabbed the brandy the footman had placed in front of him and downed it in one burning gulp. Damn it all to hell. She might be of the Quality, but he still couldn't marry her. She wanted to marry for love. *Love* of all blasted ridiculous things. He could never give her that. And he couldn't very well ask Madeline to marry him on the basis of saving her reputation from Henrietta's serpent's tongue either. Madeline would only insist he didn't marry Henrietta for her sake, and he couldn't allow her to do that. He refused to tell her that he'd put her future in jeopardy again last night by kissing her, and Madeline herself had made it quite clear that she would never marry for anything other than love. He wouldn't hurt her further by offering her a loveless marriage. No. All he could offer her was sadness. A loving marriage was out of the question for him. He refused to do to Madeline what his father did to Mama. Justin couldn't bear to hurt Madeline like that. He cared about her too much. But care wasn't love and he wasn't capable of love...just like his father.

Justin had made up his mind and knew precisely what he must do. He tossed a wad of bills on the table to pay for his drinks before calling out to the nearest footman. "Have my coach brought round. I'll be leaving as soon as I have a word with the Duke of Hollingsworth."

It was after dusk by the time Justin returned home. As soon as he made it to his study, he wasted no time sending up a note to ask Madeline to meet him. She arrived not a quarter of an hour later. She knocked tentatively on the door before stepping inside. She looked beautiful and vulnerable, and his chest was tight, knowing what he had to say to her.

"Come in," he prompted.

She walked in and stood in front of his desk, her gaze searching his face.

He took a deep breath. There would be no easy way to say this besides just getting the words out. He'd made his decision, and he intended to see it through. It was in her best interest.

"I won't apologize," he began, "for last night."

"Good. Because I don't *want* an apology," she returned.

"I'm glad to hear that. It was a special night and I'll cherish the memory of it for the rest of my life."

"I will as well." She eyed him warily. "Why do I sense the next word out of your mouth is going to be 'however'?"

Justin cleared his throat. He forced himself to meet her gaze. He'd been a rogue, a scoundrel, and a damn fool. At least now while he was making it right, he would have the courage to look her in the eye. "I have some important news. I'm…" He cleared his throat. This was more difficult than he'd expected it to be. And he hadn't expected it would be easy. "I've chosen a wife."

A flicker of something flared in her bright blue eyes. Pain mixed with surprise.

He swallowed. "And I've found you a new position. If you want it."

The furrow in her brow deepened. "Pardon?"

"The Duke of Hollingsworth has agreed to hire you as a lady's maid for his daughter. Her maid was recently taken quite ill. I will give you a sterling reference, of course."

Madeline's nostrils flared, and she clenched her jaw. "I see."

Justin couldn't stop himself. He barreled ahead with the rest of the story. "The pay will be even greater than what you make here, and I intend to give you six months' worth of wages on top of it. You'll have your own bedchamber. And from what I understand, the duke's daughter is a sweet, unassuming young woman who'll cause you no trouble."

Madeline lifted her chin. "You're sending me away?"

Breaking his eye contact with her for the first time, Justin expelled his breath and looked down at his desk. The bloody stone paper weight caught his eye, reminding him that a loveless marriage for her would be much more painful than this. This would be over shortly. A loveless marriage would last decades. "I cannot protect you here. I can't protect you...from *me*."

"I never asked you to protect me," Madeline replied woodenly.

"I've behaved abominably. You deserve much better than—"

"I believe *I* should be the one to know what I deserve, my lord. But I agree with you. If you've chosen a wife, I should go. Have you told Lady Elizabeth yet?"

He shook his head slowly. "I think it's best if I tell her *after* you leave."

Madeline nodded once more, then turned on her heel and moved toward the door.

"Wait," he called.

She stopped, only turning her head to the side to acknowledge him.

"This is for you." He pushed a small leather pouch filled with money toward the edge of the desk.

She turned around abruptly, stalked to the edge of his desk, grabbed the pouch, and rifled through it quickly.

Justin cleared his throat. "There's a letter of reference, the Duke of Hollingsworth's address, and six months' wages. If you want more, you need only ask for it."

Madeline pulled out the letter and the address card and

tossed the pouch full of money back on the desk. She leaned over, bracing her knuckles upon the top, and looked him dead in the eye. "Let me make myself clear, *my lord*. I spent the night with you last night because I wanted you, the way a woman wants a man, *not* the way a doxy looks for a payday. I'll take the new position, but I refuse to take money I didn't earn. I am *no whore*." Her tone dripped with ice, and her face was a mask of stone. She turned on her heel again and stalked from the room.

A knot twisted in Justin's gut as he watched her go. He hated that it had ended this way. But he'd be lying to himself if he thought he could keep his hands off her. They'd made the ultimate mistake last night. They'd gone too far. What could he possibly offer her except unhappiness and possibly a bastard child? No. She was hurt, but it was better this way. He'd been right all along. He wasn't cut out for love. He never would be. Emotions were messy things that caused pain.

Madeline had already allowed her emotions to get involved. She'd obviously been hurt when she'd left. She seemed angry, but he could tell underneath she was hurt. And *he'd* done that. He'd done that by allowing her to get close to him. By touching her. By spending the night with her.

He'd made a dozen mistakes when it came to Madeline, but at least he could do the right thing now. He hadn't told her he was planning to marry Henrietta Hazelton. It would only cause her to ask questions. Questions he didn't intend to answer. But he could provide Madeline with a better opportunity than the one she had in his household. He'd spent the entire afternoon talking to men at the club, trying to discern which household would be the best fit and provide the best accommodations for her. Hollingsworth's had sounded like the most agreeable position.

Justin didn't expect Madeline's thanks. It was the least he could do after he'd taken advantage of her. Of course, he understood why she'd refused his money, but he'd had to offer it to her. She'd refused it like a queen. He didn't blame her for that either, but regardless, sending her away from his household was for her own good. She would realize that eventually. And he would spend the rest of his life trying to assuage his relentless guilt.

CHAPTER TWENTY-SEVEN

Back upstairs in her bedchamber, Maddie tossed her belongings in her satchel. She didn't own much, so it didn't take long. This time, there wasn't a tear in sight. She wasn't sad…she was *furious*. She turned in a circle, wanting to take out her frustrations and hit something. She had managed to remain calm while she'd been in Justin's presence, but the moment she'd left the room, overwhelming anger had spread through her like wildfire.

How *dare* he offer her money? How *dare* he act as if he were doing her a *favor*? How *dare* he attempt to buy her off as if he were paying a common doxy? As if her presence was merely some insignificant problem to sweep under his expensive rug. He'd decided upon a wife today? *That* was interesting, given that he'd spent the night with her last night, the bastard.

And to *think* she'd fancied herself in love with him. She wasn't in love with the blackguard. The things he'd made her feel in bed had merely confused her. Muddled her thinking. He hadn't declared his love for her, had he? On the contrary, he'd chosen a wife and all but kicked her out of his household mere hours after they'd made love. Oh, Maddie knew it wasn't as if he could have fallen to one knee and declared himself to her, but it stung to hear that he'd chosen a wife so quickly after sharing such intimacy with her.

She spun around in one last circle, frustrated by a lack of punchable objects, before finally dropping to the bed and expelling her breath in a thwarted huff. She *was* angry with Justin…for how he'd treated her, for how he'd handled it, but she truly had no one to blame but herself. She'd made a mistake playing with fire, and now she had to suffer the consequences of that mistake.

She was fortunate, actually, that he hadn't forced her out without a reference or a new position. But even as she had that thought, she knew Justin would never do that. He was too kind. That's why she'd *thought* she'd fallen in love with him.

She might not have taken the money, but she wasn't a *complete* idiot. She would take the position at the duke's house. Besides, Justin was right. She *did* need to get as far away from him as possible. She probably should have taken the money, too, but she'd die before she allowed herself to feel like a whore. She still had her pride. She didn't need his guilt money.

She would start fresh. No more playacting or dances in the moonlight with handsome gentlemen. No more ridiculously good-looking marquesses who kissed you. The Duke of Hollingsworth was an old, married man. There was absolutely no chance of repeating her mistakes in his employ.

Once her bag was fastened, she took a brief look around the room she'd lived in for the last two months. She would miss it here. For more reasons than one. She sat down at the writing desk and penned a short missive to Lady Elizabeth. She couldn't bring herself to talk to her mistress face-to-face, and Justin was probably right. Lady Elizabeth shouldn't know until after Maddie was gone. She suspected Lady Elizabeth wouldn't be happy and would either insist she stay or insist she talk to her brother, and Maddie couldn't do either thing. No. It was better this way. She needed to leave this place. She'd made more mistakes here than she cared to think about. She needed to put it all in the past.

She waited a few moments for the ink to dry on the parchment, then she hefted her satchel onto her shoulder, folded the note, and left the room, softly clicking the door shut behind her.

She stole down the back staircase to the second floor, where she peeked out to ensure no one was about. Then she hurried down to Lady Elizabeth's room and pressed the note between the doorframe and the closed door.

Then she returned to the staircase, made her way to the ground floor, and left out the servants' entrance in the back. She'd already determined that her new employer's house was not far. She would walk past the mews to the end of the next road. It would be a short walk and she could use the fresh air...even though darkness had begun to fall.

As she left Lord Whitmore's property, she lifted her head high, straightened her shoulders, and she did not look back.

CHAPTER TWENTY-EIGHT

J ustin was sitting in his study, downing yet another glass of brandy, when Eliza came marching into the room. She didn't knock. Instead, she stomped up to his desk and tossed a note atop it.

"I know why you're here," he drawled, rubbing his forehead where the devil of a headache had taken root.

"Of course you do, but still do me the courtesy of reading her note."

He grabbed the paper with his free hand and scanned it.

> *Lady Elizabeth,*
> *I hate to leave you this way, but I have no choice. Please forgive my hasty departure. I'll always be grateful to you for your help. I wish you the best.*
> *Madeline*

Justin shrugged. "She left," he said simply, doing his damnedest to pretend as if he didn't care.

His sister glared at him, crossing her arms over her chest. "Don't pretend you don't know why she left."

He attempted to study the ledger on the desktop in front of him. Instead, the figures were a blurred mess. "What makes you think I know?"

Eliza made a scoffing sound in the back of her throat. "You're going to deny it?"

"Perhaps." He forced himself to look up at his sister.

Eliza's arms remained tightly folded. "Why else would she leave? I know something happened between the two of you last night."

"You know nothing," he insisted, ripping the quill from the inkpot and clenching it between his fingers. "She was offered a better position at another household. That is all."

Eliza's eyes narrowed. "How do you know that?"

He lifted his brows and shrugged. "We spoke."

"So you *don't* deny it?"

"Deny what?" He dunked the quill back into the pot and rubbed his aching forehead again.

His sister stamped her foot. "You're infuriating. Do you know that?"

"And *you* shouldn't pry into things best left alone." There. That was as much as he intended to say on the subject.

Eliza allowed her arms to drop to her sides, but she continued to glare at him. "You're a fool to let her go."

Justin pushed his chair back and shook his head. "Don't pretend now that you wanted a maid."

Eliza's jaw dropped. She tossed a hand in the air. "Of course I don't want a maid. I never wanted one. But you're still a fool."

Justin narrowed his eyes on his sister. "I don't know what you want from me here, Eliza. There's nothing I could offer her. She's better off far away from me. I'm sorry I cost you a maid. I shall find you a new one." He pulled his chair back toward the desk and resumed his attempt to seem as if he gave a bloody hell about his blasted ledger.

"Fine. There's only one thing left to do." His sister turned and stomped from the room.

Justin glanced up and stared at the empty space where Eliza had stood. He deserved that diatribe. Every bit of it. But he couldn't explain to his younger sister what precisely had happened between himself and Madeline and why it was so serious. It would be entirely inappropriate. Though that wasn't Eliza's fault. It was his. *All* of this was his fault. He'd been a fool and both Madeline and Eliza were suffering because of it. If only he hadn't danced with Madeline last night. If only he hadn't touched her, hadn't taken her into his arms. But it was too late now. He'd made the ultimate mistake, and he'd been forced to make things right. He didn't expect Eliza to understand that it was better this way.

He pressed his lips together as he continued to contemplate the empty doorway. What the hell had Eliza meant by her last words, *there is only one thing left to do now?* That was ominous. But he refused to chase after his sister and ask for an explanation. She needed time to calm down. She, too, would see that it was all for the best, eventually. He wouldn't push her to hire a new maid quickly either. That would be for the best as well.

He'd done the right thing, damn it. The noble thing. The kindest thing. So why did he feel as if he had been punched directly in the gut?

CHAPTER TWENTY-NINE

J ustin sat at the breakfast table the next morning, completely silent. He needed to tell his family that he was soon to announce his engagement to Henrietta Hazelton, but somehow the words wouldn't leave his throat.

He was still nursing the devil of a head, and Eliza clearly wasn't speaking to him. She'd barely said a word to anyone else either. Mama, obviously sensing there was something more afoot given the sudden dismissal of Eliza's maid, remained quiet as well. Jessica, true to form, chattered enough for all of them, talking about the latest *on-dits* of the *ton,* seemingly oblivious to everyone else's unease.

"The Shillinghams' ball is coming up," Jessica said. "I have it on *quite* good authority that the Duke of Thornbury will be there."

"How do you know?" Mama asked politely, probably more to keep the conversation going than out of genuine interest.

"Tabitha Montgomery told me that Thornbury's mama is quite a good friend of Lady Shillingham and Thornbury's mama has *specifically* asked him to attend. According to Tabitha, he would never disappoint his mama."

"That sounds promising," Mama replied, taking a bite of a kipper from her plate.

Eliza continued to glare at Justin, barely eating her food, while Justin pretended not to notice. He shoveled the contents of his plate down his throat in a concentrated effort to end the meal quickly and get the hell out of there.

"Mama," Eliza finally said. "Do you remember the Atwood family? Someone asked me about them at the ball the other night, and I couldn't quite recall."

Mama nodded and patted her lips with her napkin. "Oh, yes. It's quite a sad story. Lady Atwood died leaving behind her husband, the baron, and two young daughters. Then, not ten years later, the baron died as well. Consumption, I believe. Just awful."

"Oh, that *is* sad," Jessa said, frowning.

"And that's not all," Mama continued. "When their father died, a hideous cousin arrived from the country and claimed the barony. Apparently, he offered to marry the eldest girl. When she refused, he tossed them both out of the house."

Justin scowled. "What sort of arse would do such a thing? Why didn't the father ensure his daughters were provided for?" he couldn't stop himself from asking.

"He did, apparently," Mama continued, "but the hideous cousin wasn't meant to inherit. The man the baron thought would inherit had unexpectedly died in an accident not long before the baron passed away."

"Well, *that's* positively horrendous," Jessa interjected, a sad look on her face.

"I quite agree," Eliza replied, tapping a finger to her lips. "Hmm. The story is coming back to me now. I seem to recall it after all."

"Disreputable bastard," Justin murmured, pushing

grumpily at his plate. In his current mood, he was considering finding the new baron in question and punching him dead in the face for his behavior.

"Last I heard, the elder daughter found work as a lady's maid in London," Mama finished.

"Oh, she did?" Eliza asked, a catlike smile on her face as she locked eyes with her brother. Without dropping her gaze, Eliza continued. "Mama, remind me. Don't you recall that the eldest girl's name was Madeline?"

Justin's fork clanked to his plate. His jaw tightened. "What is the family name again?"

"Atwood," Mama replied. "Lord Atwood was the prior baron. I seem to recall the daughters were Madeline and…"

"Molly," Justin whispered as the blood drained from his face.

"Yes, I believe that's right, Justin," Mama continued. "Molly *is* her name. Do you know them?"

"I think I might." He stood from the table, dropped his napkin into his chair, and stalked from the room.

CHAPTER THIRTY

J ustin spent the day in his study staring at…a handkerchief. And not just any handkerchief. A handkerchief that Madeline had dropped on her way out the other day. He'd found it immediately after she left, and he'd considered taking it to her or asking one of the footmen to deliver it. Instead, he'd kept it. He'd tucked it in his desk drawer and now he'd put it atop his desk and was watching it as if it might do something or say something to make the madness of the past two days make any sort of sense. The only thing the handkerchief told him, however, was that he felt differently about Madeline than he'd ever felt for anyone before. For God's sake, he'd never stared longingly at a handkerchief before. What the bloody hell was the matter with him?

And what exactly had been Eliza's point, sharing the story of Madeline's past and her surname with him in that not-so-subtle manner? She obviously had no idea that he already knew Madeline was from the Quality. Even so, what did it matter?

Only, he already knew the answer to his own question.

His sister had clearly been making the point that Madeline's background meant she was suitable for him to marry. The news that Madeline was a baron's daughter changed nothing for him. Did Eliza think him such a snob? She might as well have saved her breath. He had no intention of marrying a woman who had feelings for him, and it had nothing to do with Madeline's background. He also had no intention of explaining it to his sister.

"Blast all meddlesome sisters," he grumbled.

A sharp knock at the door was followed by it swinging open and Veronica marching in. She wore a fashionable ruby-red gown and had her gloved hands planted on her hips.

"There you are," she blurted, striding forward and taking a seat in the large leather chair in front of his desk.

"Speaking of meddlesome sisters," he mumbled under his breath.

She cupped a hand behind an ear. "What was that?"

"Nothing. You were looking for me?" he drawled. He was *not* in the mood for Veronica this evening. Not if she intended to give him hell, which he could only imagine was her intent.

"Yes, and I would very much like a drink," she replied with a smile.

Justin stood and made his way to the sideboard to pour her a glass of brandy. "I assume you'll tell me why you've come if I wait long enough," he said as he crossed back to his desk and handed her the drink.

Veronica took the glass and eyed him carefully. "I should think it would be obvious. I've come to ask you what you intend to do about Madeline Atwood."

Justin's brows shot up. "What do *you* know about Madeline Atwood?"

Veronica took a large sip of her drink before rolling her

eyes at him. "I know she's the young lady you danced with at the Hazeltons' ball last year and the same young lady you went looking for this year. I know that until yesterday she was employed as Eliza's maid. And I know she's no longer here because of something to do with you. Shall I go on?"

"No," he barked. He didn't care to hear any more and was alarmed by how much Veronica knew already. He sighed. That was the curse of growing up with three sisters and a mother. They all knew everything and told one another every detail. It was obvious. *This* is what Eliza had meant when she'd said there was only one thing left to do...set Veronica on him.

"Well," she pressed. "What do you intend to do about her?"

He took a deep breath and expelled it. "There is nothing left *to* do. She is no longer employed here."

Veronica took a sip from her glass and gave him a sweet smile. "I was hoping you'd say you intend to offer for her."

His forehead knitted together. "Offer for her? Have you gone mad?"

She arched a brow. "Oh, Justin. Don't be tedious. We both know she's the first young lady you've given a toss about in, well, ever."

He groaned and scrubbed a hand through his hair. "So that means I should marry her, then?"

Veronica took another drink. "Do you deny you have feelings for her?"

Justin expelled his breath and sipped from his own glass while he took a moment to think. Blast and damnation. A hundred thoughts chased themselves around his mind. Why had Madeline never told him she was the daughter of a baron? She'd gone out of her way to keep him from learning her surname. She'd been quick to change the subject when he'd asked. Had she not trusted him with the truth? And why did that fact cause his chest to ache more than anything else?

If her father hadn't died, she would have been here, in London, having had her own debut. She'd have been just another one of the ladies in the ballrooms that he never paid any attention to. He probably wouldn't have given her a second look. Oh, that wasn't true. There had always been something about Madeline. Something that drew him to her like a moth to a flame. Something alluring and intriguing. And baron's daughter or lady's maid—he didn't give a good goddamn which—he missed her. Desperately.

None of that mattered, of course. First, what sort of arse would he be if he asked her to marry him now? It would seem as if she hadn't been good enough for him until he realized she was a lady. A lie—she was far too good for him no matter what her station in life.

And second, and far more importantly, Madeline might be a baron's daughter, but it didn't make *him* a suitable husband. He was still the same man he'd always been. He was still the son of his awful, philandering father and nothing would change that. Nothing ever could. So, yes, he'd spent the day contemplating his options, and he'd already made his decision. A decision which he related to his nosy sister. "I'm *not* going to offer for her."

"You didn't answer my question," Veronica replied, tapping the top of her glass with a fingertip. "Do you or do you not have feelings for her?"

He stood and swiveled toward the window, downing the last of his drink. Damn it. Why wouldn't Veronica let this go? "Feelings, yes. But what do feelings amount to? Nothing. That's what. You know what Father did to Mama. I refuse to put a woman through that. Especially not Madeline."

Veronica stood and carried her glass to the window,

where she stood beside him and stared out into the darkness. "I had a feeling you would say something like that."

"You know me so well?" he said with a humorless chuckle.

She shrugged. "As well as anyone. And that's the other reason I've come."

"Why's that?" he groaned, already dreading the answer.

"You once helped me by telling me hard truths I needed to hear, and I'm about to return the favor."

Oh, no. Justin wasn't about to listen to any 'hard truths.' Absolutely not. "You can save your breath—"

"I've no intention of saving my breath." She raised her dark brow in the same manner Mama did when she wasn't messing about. "Justin, you're *not* Father and you never will be. You never can be. You're caring and thoughtful and respectful and kind. You're a good man. Father was a selfish lout."

Justin shook his head, his nostrils flaring. "How can you say that? I've spent my entire adult life indulging my every whim, including when it comes to women. *A lot* of women, Veronica. There's not a chance I'd be a good husband."

She shrugged. "So, you've enjoyed yourself as a bachelor. You're hardly the first to do so. There's no harm in that. But there's also every chance you will be a wonderful husband, when you decide to commit to someone."

Justin wanted to crush the brandy glass in his hand. "You don't know what you're talking about," he growled.

Veronica turned sharply to face him. "I most certainly do. Listen to me. I've known you my entire life. You're *not* the sort of man who'll cheat on his wife. You're *not* the sort of man who'll hurt someone you love. It's not in you, Justin. Father was a liar. I've never known you to lie. Father was a cheater. I've never known you to cheat. Father thought only of himself. I've never known you to be selfish or unkind.

You've never done any of the things Father did to hurt people around you, so why do you think you'll be like him with a wife?"

Justin clenched his jaw. His sister was slowly driving him mad. He closed his eyes. "I don't know that I won't."

Veronica placed her free hand on her hip. "I know it. Because it's like Grandpapa told me once. Love is a choice you make every day. And if you decide to love someone, you'll give her your entire heart."

Justin shook his head. "Damn it, Veronica. Grandpapa told you that because you were being a fool, refusing to reconcile with Edgefield."

Veronica looked unimpressed. "And you're being a fool now. I fail to see the difference."

"It's entirely different," he insisted.

"Tell me. Tell me how it's different." His sister blinked at him and gave him a beatific smile.

Growling, he scrubbed at his hair again. "For Christ's sake, Henrietta Hazelton has threatened to ruin Madeline."

That bit of news served to quiet his sister for a moment. She pursed her lips and narrowed her eyes. "Really?"

"I cannot share the details," Justin continued, "but suffice it to say it's not an empty threat."

Veronica appeared to contemplate that information for another moment. "It doesn't matter, if you marry Madeline, you'll save her reputation."

Justin closed his eyes and forced himself to count to five. "I *can't* marry her."

"Why not?" Veronica's hand was back on her hip.

"Because, because I—"

"Because you what? Because you love her and you're afraid of love?"

That was it. His sister had crossed the line. Justin stalked to his desk, set down his empty glass, and pulled on his coat that had been hanging off the back of his chair. "Nonsense. My situation is completely different from yours. You were already married. Already in love. I'm… I'm…" Damn it. She'd left him at a loss for words. "I'm going out," he finally barked before stomping toward the door.

He was already in the corridor when her final words met his ears. "It's too late, Justin. You're already in love too!"

JUSTIN HAD BEEN at his favorite gaming hell for the better part of two hours before he realized he was going through the motions. He wasn't even mildly interested in the game of faro he'd been playing despite the absurd amount of money he'd wagered, and he'd quickly dismissed the lovely woman who'd attempted to sit on his lap while she purred naughty things into his ear. Both things were completely unlike him.

Blast. Sitting here and losing money because his mind wasn't in the game was foolish. He folded his hand and went out to stand on the balcony and clear his head.

He strode to the balustrade that overlooked the park. He braced his forearms atop the cool stone and stared out into the darkness. He closed his eyes and blew out a deep breath. Hell and damnation, what was wrong with him?

His sister's words rang in his ears. They'd been ringing in his ears all blasted evening. He worried they might ring in his ears for the rest of his life.

You're already in love too!

He'd quickly dismissed her statement as he'd stalked out of the house earlier, but now, now, he had to wonder if there was any truth in them.

It couldn't possibly be true, could it? But if it wasn't true, what was this feeling that had invaded his every waking moment? Regret? Guilt? What was this soul-numbing fear that he'd never see Madeline again?

Love?

Was that truly what was wrong with him? Was that what he was feeling? Edgefield had described it in the past as life changing. Justin had thought that sounded fine. *For Edgefield.* After all, the man was married to Justin's sister. Edgefield had wanted a loving marriage. But Justin had never had any intention of falling in love. Love was for other people. Not a man who'd vowed he'd never hurt a woman the way his father had hurt his mother.

It had seemed simple enough. The way to keep from hurting anyone was to not fall in love with his wife or allow her to fall love in with him. Only, he had already hurt Madeline. There had been tears in her eyes when he'd sent her away. She'd been angry, too, of course, and he didn't blame her for that, but she'd also been hurt. Was that because she'd fallen in love with *him?*

Was that the reason he couldn't stop thinking about her, the reason he no longer enjoyed the sort of amusements he'd once considered his life's purpose? He was *in love* with her? Veronica seemed convinced. Veronica's other words haunted him as well. *You're not Father and you never will be. You never can be. You're caring and thoughtful and respectful and kind. You're a good man.*

Justin had never seen himself that way. He'd always seen himself as someone who could not resist temptation. He'd taken to the pleasures of London as a teen and never looked back. His father told him again and again how he was just like him. But was Veronica right?

Of course, it was true. He wasn't his father. They were two separate people. Could Justin actually make the decision to treat a wife with kindness and respect and love if he committed to her? He couldn't imagine ever cheating on

Madeline. He couldn't imagine purposely making her cry. He couldn't imagine being a selfish lout. Father *had* been a selfish lout. In more ways than one. He'd always wanted his way, insisted on his favorite meals, ensured that his decisions ruled all. Justin had never been like that. He took his sisters' feelings into consideration. He asked Mama her opinion on things. He ensured everyone in his family was happy and taken care of. Father had never given a toss about any of them. And Justin had assumed the worst about himself all these years.

He lowered his head and blew out another breath. He shook his head and uttered a humorless chuckle. Blast it. Veronica *was* right. She *had* told him a few things he'd needed to hear. God forbid he ever told her she was right, however. He chuckled again. He looked up into the dark night sky and shook his head again. By God, he'd been the biggest fool imaginable. Instead of sending Madeline away, he should have *begged* the woman to marry him.

He turned and made his way back through the gaming hell, ignoring the disappointed looks from the women he passed as he headed straight toward the door. He didn't give a toss about playing cards and charming ladies. There was only one lady he wanted to charm. He had to find a way to get Madeline back. It wouldn't be easy. He could hardly believe he was contemplating such a thing and as much as it pained him to admit—he would need his meddlesome sisters' help.

CHAPTER THIRTY-ONE

Maddie was in her spacious, private bedchamber at the Duke of Hollingsworth's house reading the latest letter from her sister. Tears had gathered in her eyes, but they were tears of joy, not sadness. Molly had refused Cousin Leopold's suit. Even with Mrs. Halifax encouraging the match. Her sister had decided she would take a position as a maid of all work for one of the wealthier families in the village instead of marrying their awful cousin. Maddie was so proud of Molly, she could shout.

I finally realized you were right all along, Maddie. Cousin Leopold only wanted to control us with his money and the promise of giving Papa's estate to our children. I'd rather work hard for a day's wage than live with his demands. You should have seen his face when I refused him. He couldn't believe it. I told him neither of the Atwood sisters were interested in his threats or intimidation. I'm quite busy these days, but happier than I've ever been, and I have you to thank for it, Maddie. You have been my example all these years. You've shown me how to stand up for myself and taught me how important it is to make my own way in this world. Now, you must promise me that you'll stop with the fanciful dream of someday giving me a debut in London. Why should I have a debut when you could not? You are my sister, and you owe me nothing but your own happiness.

Maddie folded the letter and wiped the tears from her eyes. She would always wish she could give Molly a debut, but at least her sister was safe. She was safe, and she had made the right decision. And refusing Cousin Leopold wasn't the only thing Molly was right about. Perhaps Maddie shouldn't have been trying to sacrifice her own life and happiness for her sister, but where had Maddie's pathetic attempts at finding happiness got her? In love with a betrothed marquess who had tried to pay her off and sent her away. Over the last few days, she'd examined her feelings and had come to realize that she was, in fact, in love with Justin. Despite what a fool he'd been, she loved him. She couldn't help herself, though she desperately wished she could. It was terribly inconvenient.

Maddie slid the letter into the desk drawer just as a knock sounded at her bedchamber door. She stood, crossed to the door, and opened it to see one of the duke's footmen standing there. "Begging your pardon, Miss Atwood, but His Grace requests your presence in the drawing room immediately."

Maddie pointed at herself and blinked. "*My* presence?"

"Yes." The footman nodded before rushing away.

Maddie gulped. Oh, no. She wasn't about to get sacked again, was she? She hadn't borrowed any clothing or jewelry or tried to sneak anywhere for a dance. She hadn't attempted to play the pianoforte, and she *certainly* hadn't kissed or been kissed since she'd arrived at the Hollingsworths' house a few days past. What in the world had she done now?

Maddie smoothed her skirts, glanced in the small looking glass on her desk to ensure her hair and cap were presentable, then hurried downstairs to the drawing room. The moment she stepped inside, she stopped short. There, sitting on a rose-colored sofa facing the double doors, were all three Whitmoreland sisters. The duke stood near the door. He'd clearly been waiting for her.

"Ah, Miss Atwood, there you are. I believe these ladies would like to have a word with you. I'll leave you to it." The duke quickly strode from the room, leaving Maddie blinking at Justin's sisters.

"First," Lady Elizabeth began, "I have a confession."

Maddie bit her lip. She slowly walked to stand in front of her former mistress. "Yes?"

Lady Elizabeth cleared her throat. "The night you told me your story, I promised not to share it with anyone, and I didn't. But I did manage to find a way to let my brother know who you are."

Maddie nodded. "It's all right, my lady. It doesn't matter. It's all in the past now."

Justin's third sister stood. "Second, I should introduce myself. I am Veronica Sinclair."

"You're...you are the Duchess of Edgefield, are you not?"

176

Maddie breathed. She'd seen the duchess from afar a time or two. She was always perfectly dressed. She was also as lovely as her sisters.

"Yes, and I'm Justin's sister," the duchess continued. "And we have a question for you. Then, a proposal."

"What is your question?" Maddie said in as calm a voice as she could muster.

"Are you in love with Justin?" Lady Jessica blurted.

"Jessa!" Lady Elizabeth reprimanded. "You're not supposed to say it that way."

"Why not?" Lady Jessica insisted. "This is terribly romantic, and I feel as if we should not be casual with something this important."

"You make a good point, Jessa," Lady Veronica added, tapping her cheek. "At any rate, the words are already out." She faced Madeline head-on. "Despite our lack of finesse, we would like to know…are you in love with our dear brother, Justin?"

Madeline wanted the drawing room floor to open and swallow her. "I… I…" She *was* in love with Justin, but what good would come of admitting it to his sisters? She would only make a fool of herself.

"He told me he's chosen a wife," Maddie said. There, that should be enough to silence them on the subject.

Veronica rolled her eyes. "Oh, no. *That's* a long story that I'll allow Justin to tell, but suffice it to say, the woman he would like to be his wife is most assuredly *you*."

"Wait," Lady Elizabeth interjected. "First, you need to know that we believe Justin is madly in love with *you*. In fact, we're quite certain of it."

Madeline narrowed her eyes on her former mistress. She remained entirely skeptical. "Did he *say* that?"

"Not in so many words," Lady Veronica replied, "but

sisters can tell. Mama quite agrees, too, by the by. But he *did* ask for our help. Which is why we're here."

"Help with what?" Madeline ventured, still quite skeptical.

"Help with winning you back," Lady Jessica said with a huge smile on her face. "See? Ever so romantic." She sighed.

Madeline continued to watch them carefully. She narrowed her eyes. "Winning me back as a servant?"

"An excellent question," Lady Veronica replied. "And one I would want to know the answer to as well. You're quite astute."

"No, not as a servant," Lady Elizabeth said. "In fact, his precise words were…oh, what did he say exactly, Veronica?"

The duchess cleared her throat. "His precise words were, 'I fear I've made a horrible mistake and she'll never speak to me again. Do you think she'll attend the Shillinghams' ball with me if I ask?'"

"Pardon?" Madeline's mouth fell open.

Lady Jessica nodded. "We're here to take you back and get you ready for the ball, if you'll come with us."

"Pardon?" Madeline repeated. She was entirely aware that she sounded like a fool, but she couldn't quite comprehend what they were saying.

"I'm terrible with *coiffures*, but Jessa's maid has agreed to help and she's quite good," Lady Elizabeth added.

"Yes, and I've got the loveliest lavender gown for you to wear," Lady Veronica said. "And diamond earbobs," she added with a wink.

Madeline stared at the lot of them as if they'd lost their minds. Were the Whitmoreland sisters truly sitting in her new employer's drawing room asking her to come with them and be prepared to attend a ball with Justin? "I don't underst—"

"It's simple," Lady Veronica interrupted. "Justin loves you.

He knows he made a grave mistake. He's quite prepared to grovel. And he'd like to escort you to the Shillinghams' ball tonight."

"Ever so romantic," Lady Jessica chimed in, batting her long eyelashes.

"The question is…do *you* love him?" Lady Elizabeth finished.

Maddie cocked her head to the side and stared. She still couldn't quite believe that Justin's sister was sitting in her new employer's drawing room, asking her to come with her and be prepared for a ball. But one thing Lady Veronica had said was almost irresistible. "He's prepared to grovel?"

"Yes, and I've made it clear to him it had better be quite a lot of groveling," Lady Veronica finished with a sharp nod.

Maddie crossed her arms over her chest and contemplated that for a moment. A groveling Justin? How could she possibly resist? "And you say the gown is…lavender?"

"It's gorgeous!" Lady Veronica assured her.

Wait. It wasn't that simple. "But I cannot go to a ball. I'm Lady Emily Hollingsworth's maid," Maddie pointed out inanely.

"You didn't answer the question," Lady Elizabeth said, crossing her arms over her chest and arching a brow. "Do you love him?"

"I… I…" Maddie cast about for the right words.

Lady Elizabeth stood, took Maddie by the arm, and walked to the window with her to speak privately. "I know what you're thinking, Madeline. The night you first arrived at our house you told me the story of how you refused your awful cousin, remember? You told me that night how selfish you felt you'd been. You aren't selfish. You're human. Being selfish is different from refusing something awful. You had *every right* to refuse your cousin. And you indulged in a dance with Justin at the Hazeltons' because you're a young woman with adventure and romance in your heart. There's absolutely *nothing* selfish about that either."

A lump formed in Maddie's throat. She *had* told Lady Elizabeth about refusing Cousin Leopold and feeling selfish.

"I've no idea what love feels like, mind you," Lady Elizabeth continued, "so I cannot help you answer the question. But I do know my brother, and I've never seen him as distraught as he's been in the last few days. And don't think we haven't let him squirm. We haven't told him we've agreed to help. All I can tell you is that while he's acted a complete fool, underneath, he is a very good man, and we believe he loves you with his entire heart."

Maddie's breath caught in her throat. It was suddenly difficult to breathe. Could it really be true? Could Justin love her?

"There's one more thing I want to say to you, Madeline," Lady Elizabeth continued. She turned and squeezed both of Maddie's hands. "The night you came to our house, you also told me how much you loved your sister and would do anything for her. And you said you would only marry for love. At the risk of stating the obvious, I believe you have the chance to do both now. Wanting to marry for love is not selfish. It's perfectly right. You deserve happiness, Madeline. Everyone does." Lady Elizabeth moved toward the door and gestured to her sisters to follow. "Now. We'll step outside and give you a few moments to contemplate the matter."

Maddie's tear-filled eyes met Lady Elizabeth's kind gaze. "Wait. I don't need a few moments. I already know." She turned to face all of them. "I'm madly in love with your brother. But if any of you tell him that before he's had a chance to grovel properly, I shall *never* forgive you," Maddie finished with a laugh.

A huge smile spread across all three sisters' faces at once.

"Believe me," Lady Veronica said. "We wouldn't dream of it. Now, let's go."

Maddie glanced about. "But I can't just leave. What about Lady Emily and the duke?"

"Oh, right. You *were* Lady Emily's maid," Lady Elizabeth said, threading her arm through Maddie's again and pulling her toward the door. "But now you're the Honorable Miss Madeline Atwood, Baron Atwood's eldest daughter. Don't worry. We explained everything to the duke, and he understands completely."

"He does?" Maddie asked, blinking.

"Apparently, the duke has a soft spot for romance, too," Lady Jessica announced, "which is quite agreeable of him."

"We already found another maid for Lady Emily," Lady Veronica continued. "She's upstairs getting settled in, I believe."

"You see? Now you have no reason not to come with us," Lady Elizabeth said.

Maddie glanced around at the sisters, her brow furrowed. "But how did you all know I'd come with you?"

"I didn't," Lady Elizabeth admitted. "But Veronica and Jessa insisted you would."

"We are staunch believers in love," Lady Veronica said with a sigh and a wink.

Lady Jessica nodded her agreement.

"Now, come with us," Lady Elizabeth said. "You're about to go to your first *official* ball and dance with a *very* handsome gentleman."

CHAPTER THIRTY-TWO

Many hours later, Maddie was staring at herself in the looking glass in Lady Elizabeth's bedchamber. She couldn't quite believe the reflection staring back at her. The Whitmoreland sisters had gone to great lengths to make her look like a true princess.

No doubt she appeared vain, but she couldn't stop staring at herself. Her blond hair was swept up in a lovely chignon. The hairstyle appeared artlessly arranged but had taken Jessica's maid—all three sisters insisted she call them by their first names from now on—hours to perfect. They'd applied rouge to her cheeks, kohl to her eyelids, and some sort of black goop to her eyelashes to make them appear longer.

She wore a pair of diamond earbobs loaned to her by Veronica that put Lady Henrietta's earbobs to shame and a matching diamond necklace that made her nerves jump every time she remembered it hanging around her neck. It probably cost more than Papa's entire estate in Devon. The gown Veronica had given her to wear was a work of art. Sleek lavender satin with an empire waist. It accentuated her breasts and flared out over the rest of her body. It was lined with silver ribbon and embroidered with tiny silver stars. It couldn't have been more perfect if she'd chosen it herself.

And then there were her slippers. Beautiful, shimmering silver flats with gorgeous little matching bows she couldn't stop admiring. The shoes nearly looked like glass in the shifting candlelight. She turned in a circle in front of the looking glass and laughed. "I can hardly believe it's me."

"You're absolutely gorgeous," Eliza said, clapping her hands and smiling.

"Justin won't recognize me," Maddie replied, spinning around and around.

"Nonsense. You've always been gorgeous," Jessica added. "We've merely enhanced your beauty."

"Justin knows I'm here, doesn't he?" Maddie asked. Now that the moment to see him again was near, she felt as if she might cast up her accounts. Was this real? Was she truly about to go to a London ball dressed in this finery and wearing these jewels?

"He knows and the groveling shall commence soon," Veronica replied with a certain smile. "Very soon. Let's go. It's time."

Butterflies winged around Maddie's belly as she stood and allowed the sisters to escort her out of the room and down the corridor to the second-floor landing. She stood at the top of the wide marble staircase, trembling with nerves.

"You're gorgeous and you deserve so much groveling," Eliza whispered in her ear. "Go on then."

Maddie drew a shaky breath and looked down the staircase to see Justin waiting at the bottom. She swallowed hard. He looked so handsome dressed in his fine black evening attire with a white waistcoat, shirtfront, and cravat. The exact clothing he had worn the night they'd met. An ache formed in her throat. Tears stung the backs of her eyes. There would be time to discuss everything with him later, but at the moment, she only wanted to enjoy her dream coming true. For the first time in her life—the only time— she was a debutante, about to be escorted to a *real* London ball. Oh, if only Molly could see her now. Her sister would be so shocked. Maddie would have to remember every detail to share when she got the chance.

Maddie took a deep breath and began to descend the stairs. She kept her chin carefully aloft and her shoulders straight, exactly as Mama had instructed all those years ago. She swallowed again. Mama would be so proud.

When she arrived at the bottom of the staircase, her gaze locked with Justin's. He bowed to her. "You look beautiful. No, beautiful is an inadequate word," he breathed as she placed her gloved arm on his black sleeve. "You are stunning."

"So are you," she replied with the hint of a smile. "I'm not certain how I'll be allowed in the ball without having made my formal debut, but—"

"Not to worry. We have the dukes for that," Veronica said as she and her sisters descended the staircase behind her.

Maddie's eyebrows shot up. "The dukes?"

"Yes. Come with me and allow me to introduce you to them." Justin covered her hand with his and a thrill shot through her as he led her across the foyer to the drawing room.

When the door opened, inside were two men wearing black evening clothes. One was young and handsome with dark hair and startling green eyes. The other was elderly, with a crop of white hair and a charming smile.

Justin led her to the elder of the two first. "Grandpapa, the Honorable Miss Madeline Atwood. Madeline, this is our grandfather, His Grace, the Duke of Holden."

"Your Grace." Maddie fell into her deepest curtsy.

The kindly, elderly gentleman bowed to her. "My pleasure, Miss Atwood."

She straightened and nodded, hoping she'd made a good impression on Justin's grandfather before Justin turned her to meet the *other* duke in the room.

"Edgefield, this is the Honorable Miss Madeline Atwood," Justin said. "Madeline, this is His Grace, the Duke of Edgefield, Veronica's husband."

Another deep curtsy. "Your Grace."

"No need to be formal with me, Miss Atwood," the green-eyed duke replied. He took her hand and bowed over it. "My name is Sebastian."

After Madeline insisted the duke call her by her Christian name as well, Justin escorted her over to the settee where he introduced her to his adorable white-haired Grandmama. Then, he presented her to his mother as if the marchioness had never met her as Madeline, the lady's maid, which had to be the most endearing thing ever. Both women were nothing but welcoming and kind.

Once all the introductions had taken place, Justin turned to her as if she were the only person in the room and said, "Shall we go?"

WHEN THE CARRIAGES pulled up to the Shillinghams' town house, the five-story home was brightly lit and filled with partygoers.

Maddie allowed Justin to help her from the carriage they'd shared with his mother and the twins. She threaded her arm through his as their little group made its way up to the front door.

The Whitmorelands were perfectly right. The Shillinghams' butler didn't blink when they gave him Maddie's name. As they made their way toward the ballroom doors, somehow Justin produced a bouquet of lilacs. She suspected Veronica must have had them in *her* carriage. He handed them to Maddie, whispering, "These are for you. To make your dreams come true."

Lilacs. He'd remembered the lilacs. She clutched the fragrant flowers to her side as she descended the grand staircase into the ballroom on Justin's arm.

Time slowed.

Justin was right. Her wildest dream was coming true. Pure happiness shot through her as she allowed her gaze to scan the enormous room filled with beautiful women wearing gorgeous gowns and handsome gentlemen with their snowy-white cravats. There was laughter and candle-light and music and dancing.

And *hors d'oeuvres.*

Lots and lots of *hors d'oeuvres.*

It was all *precisely* how she'd always pictured it. And tonight, she wasn't a lady's maid pretending. She was a guest on the arm of the most handsome man in the room. She closed her eyes and breathed in the simply magical air. She would remember this moment for the rest of her life.

When they reached the dance floor Justin turned to her and bowed. "May I have this dance, Miss Atwood?"

The hint of a smile curled her lips. "Isn't dancing for married men, lovesick fools, and fops?"

He took the bouquet of lilacs from her arm and handed them to Eliza, who appeared to have been waiting purposely to take them.

"Guilty," he said, offering his arm again. "You are looking at a lovesick fool."

Maddie had to swallow and shake her head to dispel the tears from her eyes. A waltz began to play. The same waltz they'd danced to in the drawing room at the Hazeltons'.

"The waltz?" She breathed, her chest going tight. "It's not a coincidence, is it?"

"Not a chance," he said, delivering his most roguish grin.

Maddie placed her hand on his arm again, and he escorted her to the middle of the dance floor. Her head was filled with clouds, and her heart was filled with light as Justin took her into his arms.

One. Two. Three.

One. Two. Three.

They spun around and around under the glowing chandeliers while the familiar waltz filled the air, and pure joy filled Maddie's heart. And for the first time in many, many years, the voice in her head telling her how selfish she was melted away. She relished every single moment of the dance.

When the music finally came to an end, Justin escorted Maddie to the refreshment table where he selected two flutes of champagne. Then he nodded toward the French doors that led out to the balcony.

"Would you care for some air, Miss Atwood?"

All Maddie could do was happily nod.

They stepped out into the soft night and the breeze caught the wisps of hair at Maddie's nape as they strolled toward the balustrade together, arm in arm. When they came to a stop, Justin handed her one of the flutes.

Maddie took a tentative sip. "This is truly a dream come true," she said with a sigh, lifting her chin in the air, closing her eyes, and allowing the breeze to caress her cheeks.

"Not quite. Not yet," Justin replied solemnly.

Maddie opened her eyes to see a recalcitrant look on his face. "What do you mean?"

"I doubt in your dreams you were escorted to the ball by a complete fool."

Maddie pressed her lips together and took another sip of

the light, crisp champagne. "I *was* told there would be groveling."

"And so there shall be," Justin said with a laugh. He took her flute and set both atop the balustrade, then he pulled one of her hands to his heart and took a deep breath. "I'm sorry, Madeline. It's not enough and it's not an excuse, but the truth is I didn't think I was the kind of man who could ever deserve your love or treat you like the treasure you are. And although I was a complete fool, I thought I was doing the right thing for you when I sent you away. I thought I was being selfless and noble. Instead, I only missed you terribly."

"You missed me?" she sniffed.

"Every second. It took my sister pointing out the fallacy of my idiotic beliefs to make me see clearly. If I could take back every single word I've said to you since we first met, I would. I would do it all again and declare myself to you and tell you how much you mean to me and beg you to marry me." He dropped to one knee, still holding her hand. "I am begging now. *Please* forgive me for being an idiot. Forgive me for sending you away, for offering you money, and for being a complete cur. I don't deserve your forgiveness, and I certainly don't deserve your love, but I'll spend every day of my life trying to earn them both. I love you madly, Madeline. And I have discovered that I simply cannot live without you. *Please* say you'll marry me."

Tears stung Madeline's eyes. She hadn't expected the groveling to make her cry. She had to take several deep breaths before she could respond. "First," she began, "I shouldn't want you to take back every word you said to me since we met. You've said some lovely things. I believe my favorite was when you told me I was the only woman you could think about."

"I'm a fool," he cursed. "I should have asked you to marry me that night. I knew then how special you were to me."

"You're not a fool, Justin." She shook her head softly. "I couldn't love a fool."

"Does that mean…?" A smile spread across his face. "You love me?"

She pulled him up into her arms and hugged him fiercely. "If I were a different person, I might ask you to grovel longer, but I cannot stand it. Yes. I love you, Justin, and yes, of course, I'll marry you."

He stepped back and looked her solemnly in the eye. "I need you to know I'm *not* asking you to marry me out of guilt or only because I've learned about your family."

"I know that," Maddie replied. "I wouldn't agree if I thought any differently."

"But I do have to ask you, my love. Why didn't you tell me who you were?"

Maddie swallowed. "I wanted the best for my sister. Letting the *ton* know I was working as a maid would have damaged her prospects."

"But Henrietta Hazelton knew," Justin prompted.

"Yes, she knew, and she held it over my head every chance she got. Paid me a pittance to keep my secret."

Justin squeezed her hands. "If you had told me, I could have helped you."

Maddie shook her head. "I couldn't have accepted your help."

"Why not?"

"You know why not. I'm far too proud for that." She laughed.

Justin nodded. "Seems we've both been stubborn. Veronica will never let me forget this, you know? Which reminds me, there's something else I must promise you. Something Veronica helped me realize."

Maddie nodded. "Go on."

Justin took a deep breath. "Trust is something earned

over time. But I promise I'll *never* betray you. And I'll aways put you first. And tomorrow morning we're going to Devon to fetch your sister. You will both live at Veronica and Sebastian's house until our wedding."

Maddie jumped into his arms and hugged him. "Truly?" she squealed.

"Yes, and Mama has already agreed to sponsor Molly next Season."

After giving Justin one more quick hug, Maddie grabbed her champagne flute and brought it to her lips. She drained it while spinning around and around in a circle under the stars. The ball and the dancing and the beautiful gown were all absolutely perfect, but in that moment, Madeline realized that *true* happiness was found with the people she loved. She would be entirely content never to set foot in a ballroom again as long as she was by Justin's side. "I've truly never been happier than this moment."

Justin waited until she stopped spinning and kissed her atop the head. "I'm glad to hear it. Let's go inside and tell Mama and my sisters we're to marry. No doubt they have their ears pressed to the French doors."

Madeline laughed. "Yes. Let's go."

No sooner had they re-entered the ballroom through the double doors, than Henrietta Hazelton appeared in front of them.

Justin cursed under his breath.

"There you are, *my lord*," Henrietta said, eyeing Maddie with obvious distaste. "I believe it's time to make our announcement." She raised her voice so that the people standing near them could hear. "Lord Whitmore is about to announce his engagement," she called.

Word quickly spread through the ballroom and after a few moments, a hush fell. Justin stepped forward and tugged at his coat. "Yes, thank you for getting everyone's attention,

Lady Henrietta," he said in a booming voice. "I would like to announce that I've just asked the most wonderful woman in the world to marry me, and she has said yes."

Cheers and well wishes could be heard throughout the ballroom.

When the noise quieted again, Justin continued, "Miss Atwood has agreed to be my bride. I am the luckiest man alive."

Henrietta's face fell, then it was covered with a look of pure rage. "I shall ruin you," she hissed at Maddie between clenched teeth. "I saw you two kissing in the drawing room."

Maddie narrowed her eyes on her former mistress. "If you say a word to anyone, I'll let the entire *ton* know you have a habit of sneaking Jimmy, the stable hand, into your bedchamber from time to time. I'm certain your *father* would like to know about it for one."

Henrietta turned white as a handkerchief and backed away quickly.

Justin grinned and pulled Maddie's hand to his lips and kissed it. "You're amazing."

"She should know better than to tangle with a lady's maid," Maddie replied. "We know *everything*."

The congratulations and well wishes continued for the better part of the next quarter hour and Justin was just about to ask Maddie to dance again when Eliza came rushing up to them.

"I'm ever so sorry to interrupt," Eliza said. "But Mama sent me to tell you that she and Jessica and I must leave. Immediately."

"Why?" Justin asked, his brow furrowing. "What's wrong?"

"It seems Jessica has just publicly slapped the most eligible bachelor of the Season."

THANK YOU FOR READING. I hope you enjoyed Justin and Maddie's story. The next book in the Whitmorelands series is *The Debutante Dilemma*. Find out why Jessica slapped the Duke of Thornbury at the Shillinghams' ball. CLICK HERE FOR The Debutante Dilemma.

ALSO BY VALERIE BOWMAN

Kiss Me At Christmas (Book 10)

Mr. Hunt, I Presume (Book 10.5)

No Other Duke But You (Book 11)

Secret Brides

Secrets of a Wedding Night (Book 1)

A Secret Proposal (Book 1.5)

Secrets of a Runaway Bride (Book 2)

A Secret Affair (Book 2.5)

Secrets of a Scandalous Marriage (Book 3)

It Happened Under the Mistletoe (Book 3.5)

Thank you for reading *The Marquess Move.*

I'd love to keep in touch.

- Visit my website for information about upcoming books, excerpts, and to sign up for my email newsletter: www.ValerieBowmanBooks.com or at www.ValerieBowmanBooks.com/subscribe.
- Join me on Facebook: http://Facebook.com/ ValerieBowmanAuthor.
- Reviews help other readers find books. I appreciate all reviews. Thank you so much for considering it!

Want to read the other Whitmorelands books?

- The Duke Deal
- The Debutante Dilemma
- The Wallflower Win

ABOUT THE AUTHOR

Valerie Bowman grew up in Illinois with six sisters (she's number seven) and a huge supply of historical romance novels.

After a cold and snowy stint earning a degree in English with a minor in history at Smith College, she moved to Florida the first chance she got.

Valerie now lives in Jacksonville with her family including her two rascally dogs. When she's not writing, she keeps busy reading, traveling, or vacillating between watching crazy reality TV and PBS.

Valerie loves to hear from readers. Find her on the web at www.ValerieBowmanBooks.com.

facebook.com/ValerieBowmanAuthor

twitter.com/ValerieGBowman

instagram.com/valeriegbowman

goodreads.com/Valerie_Bowman

pinterest.com/ValerieGBowman

bookbub.com/authors/valerie-bowman

amazon.com/author/valeriebowman

Printed in Great Britain
by Amazon